A SCABBY BLACK BRAZILIAN

SWITCH

KS-001

A SCABBY BLACK BRAZILIAN

Jean-Christophe Goddard
João Ywarete Pyaguachu

Foreword by Eduardo Viveiros de Castro

**Translated by Thomas Murphy
with Maya B. Kronic**

URB
ANO
MIC

KS-001

Published in 2023 by
URBANOMIC MEDIA LTD,
THE OLD LEMONADE FACTORY,
WINDSOR QUARRY,
FALMOUTH TR11 3EX,
UNITED KINGDOM

Originally published in 2017 as
Brazuca nagão e sebento (Portuguese) and
Brésilien noir et crasseux (French)
by n–1 ediçoes, São Paolo

Obra publicada com o apoio da Fundação Biblioteca Nacional e do
Instituto Guimarães Rosa do Ministério das Relações Exteriores do Brasil

Published with the support of the National Library Foundation and the
Guimarães Rosa Institute of the Brazilian Ministry of Foreign Affairs

Copy editor: Amy Ireland

BRITISH LIBRARY CATALOGUING-IN-PUBLICATION DATA

A full catalogue record of this book is available
from the British Library

ISBN 978-1-915103-08-6

Distributed by The MIT Press, Cambridge, Massachusetts
and London, England

Type by Norm, Zurich
Printed and bound in the UK by
Short Run Press

www.urbanomic.com

Contents

Zeno of Hylaea[1]

Eduardo Viveiros de Castro

*These bizarre shapes you see floating in the middle of the night,
in the early hours of the morning!*

Sony Lab'ou Tansi

It is first and foremost a question of knowing what *not* to write in the
prefatory atrium of this pantophagic text in which a seemingly austere
French professor of philosophy, an international authority on the work
of one João Amadeu Pinheirinho (aka Johann Gottlieb Fichte) enters
into a creative state of schizoid delirium when faced with the impossibility of domesticating the 'Brazilian condition' through the concept,
setting off on a wild divagation starting from a famous hallucinatory
episode suffered by the Iberian Jewish heretic Bento Espinosa, only to
meltamorphose it into the trance state of Descartes as depicted
in Paulo Leminski's 1965 metaphysical novel *Catatau*. Then the
author begins to shoot barbed arrows left and right, just like one
of those mythological archers in indigenous tales who only hit the
target when they are looking in another direction, in any direction
except that in which their prey lies. Sometimes the arrows miss

1. [The original Portuguese title transports the presocratic philosopher Zeno of
Elea into Hylaea (the Herodotean name given by Alexander von Humboldt to
the South American rainforest), at the same time playing on the similarity of the
Portuguese rendering of the philosopher's name, Zenão (Zeno) to *senão* (if not/
otherwise—suggesting the 'exceptional' nature of this volume)—trans.]

their mark, a doubly *necessary* outcome of every errant text.[2] But often they hit the bullseye, when the archer looks in the right wrong direction. They miss to hit, they hit when they miss. But nobody emerges unscathed from this fantastic anthropojaguaromachia. Least of all the Brazilian nation, that European idea materialised into a monstrosity that cannot be circumscribed by the *Cogito*, and which here ends up being de-totalised, in carnivalesque fashion, into a Bra-zll–1. The Brazil of the European gaze, be it that of the Europeans who came here to check it out—the preferred but not exclusive targets of these anti-christophoric arrows—or that of the many Brazilians who 'have eyes, but do not see'. Us. The others. And many another 'us' that we may or may not be bound to.

Faced with this text on the impossible-unthinkable of 'our condition', I realised that there were two approaches that had to be avoided. Firstly, furnishing the text with a critical apparatus and journalistically revealing all the sources and all the recipients of its barbs, or academicising it with abundant elucidations of the chaotically allusive material it contains. After all, if you get it, you get it. And secondly, on the contrary, allowing myself to be completely contaminated by Pyaguachu's style, something that would be (indeed, is) redundant, since the author has already plunged headlong into a parodic multiplicity of other people's voices, mixing languages and cultures, countries and continents, events and rhetorical-mimetic registers, bringing in anyone and everyone as interlocutor, inspiration, muse, example, simulacrum, friend, anti-double, enemy; he praises and curses, mocks and falls in love, swings from digression to aggression, from elegy to praise, from sarcasm to wonder, from paranoia to metanoia. He equivocates multivocally in his perverse conversion to a deliriously real Brazil. (Think of a pantheistic *Pilgrim's Progress* originally written in lowbrow Occitan and adapted by a Bahia-Baroque *Boca do Inferno* teleported into the twenty-first century. Not to mention the radicality

---

2. In Greek, *hamartanó*, 'to err', 'to commit an error', originally meant 'to miss the target [with one's arrow]'; let us disregard as irrelevant the theological-moral connotations that *hamartia* and *hamartánein* took on for Christianity.

of translation, which raises the excess of the original to an excess-and-a-half—a countercannibalisation). Anyway, in any case, 'don't try this at home' either: don't try to spoil others' pleasure, don't extract some scholastic *disputatio* from the text, falling into the debaters' trap, don't devitalise this ululating proliferation of *bare philosophy* (in the sense of 'bare life'). We shall try our utmost not to do so here.

Of course, confronted with this essay one could always say, shrugging one's shoulders and ironically rolling one's eyes, 'Here comes another goddamn Frenchman trying to explain us to ourselves; who does he think he is?' Indeed. But this essay truly veers off all the usual tracks. No longer an *interpretation of* Brazil, it is an *interpenetration* with Brazil, an attempt to think *with*, not *about* Brazil, a country as imaginary as it is real. What the author sees is the other of/in 'us', the other that we do not want to be or that we imagine we are not, even though we persist in being it behind 'our own' backs. An insurrection behind our own backs. And this voraciously unpalatable Frenchman—but wouldn't he himself be eaten up by these alter-Brazilians like a sardine (or a Bishop Sardinha), after ranting on from within our own bowels?—is jerking around with pretty much everyone here. What he tries to do is to *de-explain* Brazil and the vast world that is associated with it, one invented by Europeans, philosophers, and anthropologists (most of them French). Explanation via babelisation, via sheer mess—via the 'multiplication of the multiple', to quote Pierre Clastres, vilified by the author here, who accuses him of oedipalising the Aché, forgetting (as he has every right to do...) his own magnificent invention of the war machine against the State, so crucial for the authors of *Anti-Oedipus*.[3] An explanation, finally, spoken in a stuttering stumble,

---

3. Deleuze and Guattari are among the very few of Pyaguachu's colleagues to whom *A Scabby Black Brazilian* does not deliver a serious slap in the face. They are translated here as Oswald and Guaraci, and/or F[r]anny (Deleuze) and Dina (Lévi-Strauss). Let us mention in passing that Gilles Deleuze—or Egídio da Azinheira, as he is rendered in Portuguese—received Clastres's Aché-Guayakí ethnography in a completely different way to Pyaguachu. See 'Indians Recounted with Love' [1972] in G. Deleuze, *Letters and Other Texts*, ed. D. Lapoujade, tr. A. Hodges (Cambridge, MA: MIT Press, 2020), 192–94.

stammering, *en bafouillant* as they would say in the author's native language. *Bafouiller, béaba-fouiller*—to rummage around for your ABCs. Stammering-rummaging through the analphabetomegastupidity of all languages. A different type of Frenchman therefore, one in the process of becoming-Indian-Black ('Every time an ogan hits the atabaque and calls the orisha, a Frenchman falls into a trance', says a friend of mine who is a specialist in ethnic heterogeneity), against the Whites from here and there alike. And against himself first of all, of course. His orisha possessed him. He put on a feathered headdress. He plunged deep into the caatinga.

I have not been able to resist getting just a little bit infected myself, as you can see, nor have I been able to stop myself from loosing a sneaky arrow of my own. In my defence, I submit that I am an accomplice of J.Y. Pyaguachu; after all, I was the one who dreamed up *diferOnça*, one of the anti-concepts that propels his errant text, as well as having introduced him to Oswald and Clarice and lent him *Catatau*, one night in Botafogo. 'I came here because I was called.' But it would hardly be a good look for me to claim that *A Scabby Black Brazilian* is a mere involution or appropriative reimplementation of *diferOnça* (and of the païdeuma it more or less explicitly identifies with), given the numerous other inspirations of this text, emanating from so many other sources. Let's move on.

The scabby black Brazilian of Espinosa's fleeting vision is the fuse that detonates Pyaguachu's Leminskian bomb: Olinda-Holland, the Batavian but above all Indian, Black, and Sephardic Pernambuco, whose burning, perpetually *naturans* nature drives all analytical geometry to distraction and assails the imagination of an imaginary Descartes by means of multitudes of rogue geniuses materialised in the form of phytozoomorphic chimeras. *Catatau*'s rationalist philosopher is revived here in the form of one of his most illustrious and most traitorous disciples, Spinoza, dressed up in Deleuzean drag as Artaud-Heliogabalus. Spinoza is at once the author's interlocutor and his mask, a bit like Clarice Lispector's dialogical or authorial ghosts in *The Passion According to G.H.* and *The Hour of the Star*—who are the inverted correlate of the inaudible White, that is to say Guimaraes

Rosa, listening, notebook in hand, to the daydreams and escapades of gay jagunços and cannibalistic curibocas possessed by a becoming-jaguar, an instantaneous, infinitive *déjà-guar*, tragic warriors of the oncesca matrianarchy of Pindorama. And on top of the neoplatonising Rosa of Minas Gerais and the Pernambucan Jew Lispector, the most radical Brazilian Spinozan thinker (Rosa is a fox, but Clarice is a bomb), there hovers the moustachioed silhouette of the dipsomaniacal Afro-Polish karateka who gave birth, in the highly improbable Curitiba, to the monstrous *Catatau*, an unreadable book, an anti-romance, a tropical *Finnegans Wake.* It's bad luck (?) for us that it was written in (im)Portuguese, just as it was bad luck for Joyce, that scabby Irishman (who Virginia Woolf despised, calling him 'a self-taught working man'; 'a queasy undergraduate, scratching his pimples'), to have had to write in English. But Joyce took revenge and anthropophagically crushed the language of the coloniser, taking it as the point of departure and departing from it to generate a glossolalic and polyamorphous metamyth that subverlated (sublated and subverted) another, earlier myth, that of Ulysses, doubly closing the cycle 'from myth to novel' (Dumézil, Lévi-Strauss) with a circular and intensively infinite myth, an Amazonian *riverrun*. A drunken Celtic hero, Finn, taking the place of the Homeric hero, the emblem of cunning Eurometaphysical Greekness. The director Glauber Rocha, among others, has bathed in this *riverão*, and makes an honourable appearance in Goddard's *Navilouca* of world thinkers in a pindoramic-sertanejo key.

The sertão, the hinterland. Pyaguachu finds sertão-Brazil in the Fanny-Deleuzian France of the Plateau des Millevaches and the Cévennes: 'a Brazil within France' to be set against the fin-de-siècle France that Lévi Strauss sees in the Rio de Janeiro of the 1930s and the operetta-like 'sociological minuet' that he sees in bourgeois São Paulo. Lévi-Strauss understood nothing of the country he had landed in: he overhastily rationalised Brazilian 'society'—tropical nature exceeded the threshold of his sensibility. To him Guanabara Bay was 'a toothless mouth'. Cariocas, even anthropologists and structuralists, will never forgive him for this lack of education about stone and by stone...although his sarcastic characterisation of the

São Paulo scene and the Mesquitan State University does not seem to us entirely inaccurate. But as far as Goddard is concerned, the French professor was just passing through. He operated a memorable erasure of his better half in *Tristes Tropiques*, and blocked any possibility of becoming-woman from his writing. To him the tropics seemed *triste*, when in fact they were, and are, beyond joy and sorrow—although this still has to be proved the hard way, time and time again. 'A whole people crammed into a wine-press, singing as they bled'.[4] Had Spinoza toiled in a seventeenth-century sobrado in Recife we would have a completely different Part Three of the *Ethics* today. Of course, Lévi-Strauss did far more and far better than just badmouthing the tropics; but there's no need to pick a quarrel (Lévi-Strauss must be read in the light of Oswald de Andrade, thereby allowing us to discard his old-fashioned side—ultimately just one aspect of his work). Pyaguachu's problem is a different one—and anyway, bias is his forte. He follows another thread, is part of another lineage: that of the foreigners who have come to terms with the other Brazil, indigenous, Black, caboclo, southern from head to toe. Pierre Fatumbl Verger ('Pierre Verger', literally 'Pedro Pomar' in Portuguese, a curious onomastic coincidence), Curt Nimuendaju Unkel, Gisèle Omindarewa Cossard-Binon.... The exiles, the deserters, those who did not return, those who became one with the intensive infinity of the always supraorganic and infra-organic life of Pindorama, the liana forest and the stone, the rhizomatic forest and the smooth space of the sertão, the terreiro and the terrain.

And of course let us not forget Céline, another lighthouse in the tempest of Pyaguachu's 'textão', a faithful advisor. Céline, Racine's counter-rhyme: the writer of the rhizome (..., ..., ...) against the writer of the root. The Frenchman of the *Grand Siècle* dressed as a Greek and reciting Alexandrines is no better (from rhizome to risible) than the Indian dressed as a senator of the Empire featured in the 'Cannibal

---

4. '*Tout un peuple entassé dans un pressoir saignait en chantant.*' Apollinaire, *L'Enchanteur pourrissant* [1909]—stolen from one of the epigraphs of Jorge de Lima's *Invention of Orpheus* [1952].

Manifesto'—or the cannibal *manifested*, in Beatriz Azevedo's re-adjectivised version; *the* founding text of the 'only original Brazilian philosophy' (Augusto de Campos). Céline…, …, …, the perverse genius of anti-Racinian language, the greatest innovator in the French tongue since Rabelais, with his furious tirades drawn from the depths of the trenches: 'No-one loves roses more than generals. Everyone knows that.'

Goddard, the *immobile* deserter, the non-voyaging clairvoyant who is afraid of flying (but who isn't?), the one who gets drunk on a glass of water—Henry Miller, as quoted by former boozer G.D. ('I drank a lot…'), coincidentally the greatest French philosopher of the twentieth century, who also never travelled and who, as Pyaguachu once told me, never invented anything but stole everything from others—including, above all, what no one, including themselves, knew they had—and from this plundering extracted a string of brilliant insights. Philosophical anthropophagy. Just like our author here.

Then there is the presence of Bruce Albert and Davi Kopenawa Yanomami's *The Falling Sky*, which returns *Tristes Tropiques* to sender. The shaman against the philosopher, the oneirism of the figure against the onanism of the concept. It gives us everything we need, *except perhaps [senão]*—just the one tiny fragment of mosaic missing from this ethno-schizoid frieze that has everything—Sousândrade. Taking him down a peg or two, that quiet visionary who turned romantic discourse upside-down and occupied Wall Street long before the slogan was coined; who ate the stones of his fazenda—stone chewing…. That Inca Swedenborg who dekantianised Hyperborean metaphysics with his *Tatuturema*, the cannibal hymn of the invincible *Hiléia Amazônica*. Zeno of Hylaea…our *senão*, the exception…. But I'll stop here. Be amazed.

ergo sum, aliás, Ego sum Renatus Cartesius, cá perdido,
aqui presente, neste labirinto de enganos deleitáveis, —vejo o mar,
vejo a baía e vejo as naus. Vejo mais. Já lá vão anos III me
destaquei de Europa e a gente civil, lá morituro. Isso de 'barbarus—
non intellegor ulli' —dos exercícios de exílio de Ovídio é comigo.
Do parque do príncipe, a lentes de luneta, CONTEMPLO A CONSID-
ERAR O CAIS, O MAR, AS NUVENS, OS ENIGMAS E OS PRODÍGIOS
DE BRASÍLIA

ergo sum, alias, Ego sum Renatus Cartesius, lost over here,
present over here, in this labyrinth of delightful deceptions—I see
the sea, I see the bay and I see the ships. I see more than this. It
has been III years since I left Europe and the civilised world, where
they were *morituro*. The 'barbarus—non intellegor ulli'—from Ovid's
exile exercises—that's me. From the Parque do Príncipe, through
the lens of a telescope, I CONTEMPLATE IT ALL, EXAMINING THE
QUAY, THE OCEAN, THE CLOUDS—THE ENIGMAS AND WONDERS
OF BRAZIL

Paulo Leminski, *Catatau*

Bento de Espinosa

In the year MDCLXIV, just over a century after the Caeté Indians had
butchered and devoured Brazil's first Portuguese bishop—that delicious feasting upon Bishop Sardinha that Oswald de Andrade would
go on to celebrate as the founding act of modern Brazil—the Portu-
guese-Jewish philosopher Bento de Espinosa (whose family had been
exiled to Amsterdam, the world capital of colonial trade, along with
so many other Jewish families who would soon go on to populate the
Brazilian Nordeste) wrote a letter to the most wise and prudent Peter
Balling in which he told his friend of a peculiar visual hallucination he
had suffered: the image of a 'scabby black Brazilian', which persisted
upon awaking, and returned vividly whenever his attention wandered.
He was also keen to point out that he had, good god, never seen this
figure before. Bento was replying to a letter Peter had written to him
to ask what could explain a premonitory hallucination he had had of
his late son's dying sobs, before the child had even fallen ill. Now,
everything leads us to believe that if this Bento (who also called himself Benedictus, and has entered the bibliographers' pantheon under
the name 'Benedictus de Spinoza') was so concerned about this affair
with the hallucination and took such pains to reply to Peter, it was
largely with the intention of setting his own case clearly apart from
that of his friend. In Balling's case, paternal love had conferred upon
a father the psychic power to see events in the life of his precious

son before they had taken place. Whereas Bento's hallucination involved nothing but the retinal persistence of a dream image carried over into the waking state, the effect upon his imagination of a banal physiological disturbance, like a delirium caused by fever. We reassure ourselves as best we can. It is true that white people such as this Benedictus have long since lost their ancestors' ability to see the Yanomami xapiri who accompanied Omama during his European exile, after he had fled the rainforest on the strength of a silly rumour. If Kopenawa is to be believed, these xapiri are far more beautiful than those of the Amazon rainforest. In any case, it's a fact: fantastic beings still appear to the Whites. And they don't know what to make of these strangers, to whom they willingly extend the hospitality of their own universe of thought, but from whom they learn nothing. As, over time, this Bento came to enjoy a certain renown, the clergy, disquieted by the correspondence, became involved in the matter—to tell the truth, they were somewhat embarrassed. Keen to divert the attention of the literate public away from this Brazilian's rude irruption into a philosopher's bedroom, they wondered whether Bento's explanation of the father's hallucination was in accordance with the TRUE doctrine of the man they now called 'Spinoza': whether it was TRULY Spinozist. They wondered whether perhaps Benedictus had become a little confused in his eagerness to comfort his friend Peter, to reassure him that it didn't matter that he hadn't got up that night, the night he had heard the sobbing, because the sound was imaginary, and he had heard it out of love. There's no need to go into the minutiae of the debates, which at one point even pitted a Paduan activist against the Sorbonne. 'Spinoza' had won out over Espinosa. Benedictus, the great scholar in Northern European garb, the savant of the Cold Lands, had managed to erase the very memory of Bento. Ask the first associate professor you meet if they've ever heard of Bento de Espinosa, you'll see! In dropping the first syllable of his name and forging from scratch the three syllables of the new name which would henceforth serve to summon up his spectre, was Benedito trying to relieve himself of the toponymic burden that had encumbered his people since their expulsion from Spain—was he attempting to definitively erase all memory of that idiotic Peninsula where Jews had been made to eat pork? Who knows. In any case, no connection would now remain between the Great Luso-Dutchman, fully sedentary, a part of the World's intellectual heritage, and the many peoples of Brazil, Mexico, Ecuador, and Chile who still bear the name Espinosa; no connection to all those Jews who, rather than placing themselves under the protection of the Old World, of Europe and the Mediterranean, had fled across the Atlantic to the hinterlands of the New World to lay down their burden of thorns or even, like Heitor Antunes—another Bento, a Brazilian anti-Spinoza—to plant it in the ground so as to cultivate the flowering of a New Espinosa in Minas Gerais. When Bento had received and replied to Peter's letter, he had been living in the heart of the very community which, out in Recife, had just build Kahal zut Israel, the first American synagoque from which, after the Dutch wore driven out of Pernambuco, twenty or so fellow believers would set off to found the Jewish community of New Amsterdam. A future citizen of New York, already a citizen of a Dutch New York, like all the Dutch Sephardim whether in Recife or Amsterdam, Bento could not have failed to have been entranced by the great American adventure. Associated with the colonial government by Jean-Maurice de Nassau-Siegen, on both sides of the Atlantic his people had taken part in the development of the Dutch West India Company. Amsterdam had offered them more than freedom of worship, more than a taste of the historical, political, and religious anomaly of seventeenth-century Holland: it had offered the savage power of a becoming-global which, in a manner as violent as it was aberrant, put the coasts of Europe, Africa, and America, their peoples, their kings, their languages, their religions, and their sounds into communication with one another. Restoring to their forced dispersal something of the sacred dimension of Diaspora, America plunged them into a new melting pot of seeds and blood. No wonder that, in the wee small hours of the morning, Bento was hallucinating the haunting image of a scabby black American! A visitation by a phantastic Brazilian! And more often than he admits to Peter, at that. All of which Benedictus de Spinoza would have convinced his learned bio-bibliographers to put out of their minds so that they could focus exclusively on the subtle theories of imagination and participation in essences that the philosopher distilled so as to explain the auditory hallucination of the most wise, most prudent, and very White Peter Balling. Focus on that, not on the visual hallucination of an African-American by the Sephardic Bento de Espinosa—the mere retinal persistence of a dream image, a superficial ocular disruption. But scholars can't just do as they please. The famous letter, complete with its embarrassing confession, had already been published in the philosopher's Complete Works. And nothing in the Works could escape Critique. So the critics had to find *something* to write about the Brazilian. Since Bento spoke of him as an Ethiopian, they inevitably imagined a Black man, because in Greek, that dead language of scholars, 'Ethiopian' means 'people with burnt faces': scabby black people. The morning hallucination then took on the aspect of a terrible and thrilling apparition. Terrible and thrilling for a schoolboy, that is. It became the *Erscheinung* of the unimaginable image, the image of the Black Double, the forbidden, repressed image of what the Great Philosopher Is not—of what, moreover, generally speaking, IS NOT. Spinoza before he existed, Spinoza in the *Abgrund*: Spinoza the Falasha, the Jew, the Negro. Since in Amharic (because the schoolboy also knows many living languages, especially their insults) 'falasha' is what an Ethiopian calls a Jew to remind him that he is an immigrant, the appearance of the scabby black Brazilian was naturally understood as that vision of oneself that threatens every Jew in exile via the interpellation of the Other, the goy who, as he passes, spits 'dirty Jew' in his face and, jostling him, tells him, as happened to Freud's father, to get off the pavement and back into the filthy gutter where he belongs. But this is just another way of trivialising the hallucination, of whitewashing it: relating it to the universality of the formlessness, the filth or shit which the Other piles on the immigrant's head, and which is so closely linked to the genitals, placed *inter urinas et faeces*, so that this insult thrown at him, 'dirty' or 'scabby', also casts aspersions upon his sexual hygiene. At which point there is no longer anything Brazilian, anything specifically Brazilian, about the hallucination of the scabby black Brazilian, nothing to do with the Luso-Dutch colonisation of America, but only the universal interplay of the identity and mimetic mechanisms that prevail in Europe and everywhere that Europe spreads itself: the reduction of a scapegoat to the formless pulp of a body mangled by stoning. All with the best of intentions, though, the gist of it being that Bento had done well not to have let himself be insulted by the goyim and to have given himself his own nickname, a clean white nickname coupled with the Latin first name of a saint, so that no one would suspect that he had shit all over his head and had pissed himself. So that everyone could see that you can be Jewish without being filthy and scabby— that you can be Jewish and White.

Franny Deleuze

Whether or not to treat Spinoza like a dead dog was actually a serious question for European philosophers, and in some cases, as with Hegel, who feared being mistaken for Spinoza, a genuine source of anxiety. After all, the worst thing that can happen to a philosopher in love with absolute being is to end up in the same gutter as a Jew. The fear of formlessness, of ending up with nothing more than a gaping mouth or hole, a dark abyss into which all differences sink, is always linked to the confused fear of soiling oneself and the public denunciation that would necessarily follow. Accused by his own peers of having dissolved the world into the undifferentiated, the philosopher feels as abject as the man who walks through the city with his face covered in filth, offered up unreservedly to the heinous scorn of the bourgeois. This is why he is so concerned about his reputation. He measures the value of his work by the respect he receives in the street. Anyone who aspires to a career in this field, although they may not be scabby and filthy to start with, will always face the possibility of a sudden fall into the muck of the gutter. For philosophers are no more prepared to give way to those who would take the same path as them than Christians are wont to share their pavement with a Jew. It's an old story, one that carries with it a specific Mediterranean and Greco-Latin distribution of the roles of friend and foe, the pure and the impure, origin and existence, and their relationship to the body and its orifices, especially the mouth and anus, and, so nearby, the genitals, all understood as organs of death and indifferentiation. An old story that is of no help in understanding Bento's schizophrenic American hallucination. Perhaps only a philosopher so in love with his wife that he gave her the name of a Salinger character as a nickname knows what schizophrenia is. How it is fabricated. It's not enough to just have a psychiatrist friend. You need a woman from an American novel, an American woman, in order to know that schizophrenia is an American affair, an uncommon capacity to experience those gigantic, out-of-control movements which, on the scale of universal history, create monstrous passages between continents and races, cultures and societies, mixing their destinies and concepts to the point of accomplishing real transformations, creating unknown beings that can no longer be explained by any of the categories with which Europe sets out what is possible and what is not. The humid tropical rainforest hallucinates, in Brazil, the Great African Lords of the quilombos— soul healers, fantastic psychiatrist-sovereigns of authentic Black, indigenous Bantu kingdoms—who invent new enchanted lands of exile for Jewish outcasts and all the fugitives who were once pushed into the same gutters. It creates legendary beings, beings as aberrant as Felipe Camarão, the Potiguara Templar, the Latinised native, elevated by the Portuguese to the rank of Commander of the Order of Christ for having stood at the head of an indigenous army and driven the Batavian forces out of Pernambuco. Positioned at the edge of the prodigious movements he has provoked, yet drawn toward them at the same time, swept along by their unpredictable and chaotic whirlwind, and stationed behind them, apart from them, simultaneously observing and affected by their margins, in a curiously unstable station, in tension, simultaneously dynamic and static, the colonist can see only through the hallucinatory eye of the Forest itself: giants, disproportionate, exuberant, monumental beings, Henrique Dias, Ganga Zumba, Zumbi. This is the point of view of the Brazilian, of every Brazilian, because every one of them is and remains a coloniser, a permanent coloniser, always situated in this same place, at the edge of colonial space: mata, sertões, chapadas or veredas. From this vantage point he continues to observe the anarchic movements of the heterogeneous groups that populate Brazil and is continually affected by them: bandeirantes, hunters of men and gold, insurgent armies of runaway slaves and Afro-Indian royal troops, vengeful hordes of poor peasants, jagunços and cangaceiros, the enlightened army of the rebel peoples of Canudos, urban gangs from the favelas. No national history, no instituted order of time will succeed in separating out and organising these packs of men who, by plunging social states and ethnic groups into the same melting pot of blood and sperm, connect all eras to one another, and traverse colonial space as the only anachronic site in the world, that absolute site where all human eras communicate. Does the term 'Jagunço' not originally refer to an African weapon—the same bamboo spear which, in Guararapes, won Camarão and Dias their victory against the Dutch, who were unable to use their firearms? Rocha's cinema shows this enough for those who want to see through Glauber's eye, the eye of the believer: in spite of all the efforts of the religious and political authorities to expose the corpses and date the deaths, the Brazilian continues to hallucinate royal, messianic figures who crystallise these aorgic cross-roads of revolutionary uprising and retrograde fanaticism; Antonio Conselheiro or Lampiao. Figures as violent as Rocinha's Bem-Te-Vi, otherwise known as Erismar Rodrigues Moreira, whose criminal but popular reign still has a hint of the glory of the honourable bandits of the sertão, revived on the hills of Rio where the Canudos warriors moved to, taking the Morro da Favela with them. A gang leader named after a bird? No, because 'bem-te-vi' was already a nickname for the great kiskadee; the gangster shares a nickname with a bird. A curious alliance with the animal, just as the stateless city clinging to the hill forms a curious alliance with the vegetal, with a toxic and medicinal bottleplant shrub from the sertão: the favela. But this is not just any bird: this omnipresent passerine, so pervasive that wherever you hear its song, whether in the streets of Urca or the veredas of Minas, it always seems to be the same bird, singing the same *bem-te-vi* which, if Guimarães Rosa is to be believed, the jagunço hears as a disap-proving 'I've seen you, I know what you're doing!', a persecutor accus-ing him in advance of crimes he has not yet committed. Bem-te-vi de Rocinha, a young favela king with golden pistols, an ubiquitous bird from a garden planted with flowers that existed elsewhere in another era. Yes, because these extravagant movements of peoples who dance within colonial space in defiance of all good order and progress, and who move whole blocks of territory with them and undo all reasonable correspondence and all reasonable violence between ethnic groups and classes, also abolish the boundaries between the human and the nonhuman which territorial, cultural and social identities are, in the final analysis, primarily intended to protect. For centuries, the colonist who remained at the first quay where he landed has continued to gaze inward, from the coast, at all these furious multiplicities of the hinterland and the unbuildable slopes of Rio. The bay he has inhabited for so long is still the bay where he landed, where he stands and where he ceaselessly recreates himself. Anyone who has not experienced the discovery of America, its invention, cannot understand it: it is not true here that the 'there' (as the Germans say) from which existence bursts forth and opens up a world is not a place, a birthplace, a place where being-there, precisely in that place, entails being submerged by existence. *Cais*: when Elis Regina and Milton Nascimento invent a jetty and an ocean, it is not to set sail, to flee the country, but to return to it, to return to the coastline where the lonely, melancholic European, poor in existence and in world, is reunited with the heterogeneous hordes of Brazil. The coastline is as much the border of the sea as that of the land: if the sertão one day becomes sea, the Atlantic Ocean, and the ocean becomes the sertão, it will be thanks to the coastline, to the enchantment of this cosmogonic boundary. Anyone on this shore can quite rightly be accused by the bem-te-vi of all the crimes of Brazil. Anyone (and there are some out there!) who still believes that the progressive carioca of the uptown districts have no direct involvement in the murders perpetrated by all the gangster lackeys in Brazil since the early days of colonisation, not to mention those (worse still!) they are still planning, has understood nothing.

Dina Lévi-Strauss

No European can disembark for the first time in Rio without being
exposed to the perils of such well-being. Even Lévi-Strauss only just
managed to escape it. This future academician from the quays of the
Seine where, since the days of Brazilian New Holland, France has
fastidiously preserved its cultural treasures—artists, moralists, writers, architects, politicians, etc.—once they have dried up, this young
Parisian ethnographer who had come to Brazil to gather raw material
for his books—undocumented codes of marriage, lists of clan names,
etc.—had no other destination than the Compagnie des Transports
Maritimes liners, to which he hastened to return after docking in the
New World for the first time in Rio de Janeiro, where there was nothing to see but a sort of museum of old-fashioned French provincial
or working-class Parisian urbanism: Nice or Biarritz at the end of the
nineteenth century, Neuilly, Saint-Denis, or Le Bourget at the beginning of the twentieth. Travelling from Rio de Janeiro to Santos, the
coastline would have been close enough for him to have been able
to spot, on the crestline of the coastal mountain range, the tracks
that brought gold from Minas, Ubatuba, Parati, São Sebastião, and
the improbable beaches of Barra do Sai and Camburi at the foot of
the Serra...all to no avail. But everything changes when he arrives in
Santos. As the boat reached the port, slowly making its way between
the verdant islands, the French scientist finally registered the first

shock of the tropics. Here, no more comparisons are possible. Enveloped by the copious vegetation of a forest populated by behemothic plants, one is returned to the primordial, to the dawn of creation where everything is inconceivably acute and verdant. No more comparisons, no more analogies, no more proportional correspondences, no more geographical or historical classifications, no more differences in cycle or rhythm: the rainforest can only be compared to another rainforest, the hinterland of Santos to the Amazon basin, Brazil to Brazil. And when the scholar nevertheless does attempt a comparison with what he calls 'our forest', contrasting the dark foliage and light trunks of the tropics to the light foliage and dark trunks of 'our country', the beautiful chiasmus is tarnished by peculiar evocations, which, suggesting secret passages between different realms, end up derailing the comparison: the qualities of the minerals whose traffic we were following just now are used to describe the shades of the plant, which seems to be made of jade or tourmaline; the brightness of the trunks is that of animal bones, and the stems seem to be cut out of sheet metal. By inverting the distribution of light and dark that governs the relationship between foliage and trunks in the Old World, the tropical forest operates more than a mere permutation: it changes in nature, becoming mineral and animal. The ethnographer, transformed in spite of himself into an explorer of the New World, is forced to admit it: it is 'of a different order from the Nature we know'. The shock had set in: having come in search of isomorphisms, the Frenchman was suddenly confronted with beings that could not be explained by the interplay of combinations and logical transformations. But he also resisted valiantly. Valiantly and symptomatically. To round things off, he concludes his account as follows: 'as in the landscapes of the Douanier Rousseau, beings attained the dignity of objects'. And there you have it. That's how, once you've returned to your Parisian arrondissement, you can excuse yourself, and justify not having followed up on the disturbing experience of the unknown beings of the Forest which, caught up in real transformations, seem to attest to an illogical communication between the animal, the vegetable, and the mineral. To quote 'Le Douanier' Rousseau is to admit that the picture was not complete, that the Forest still contained a scene absent from the story, for almost all of Rousseau's painted 'jungles', which restore to the animals caged in the Bois de Boulogne's Jardin d'Acclimatation the magical power of their life in the wild, are actually ritual scenes of combat and the devouring of one creature by another. Myth versus ritual, structure versus that moment of indiscernibility created by the Black man's fight to the death with the Indian jaguar—a central figure in the popular sculpture of Minas Gerais which speaks of the mysterious power of the dreaded inhabitant of the forest, possessor of the shamanic power to transform one species into another and to vary the intensity of humanness, to initiate the logical human into other, non-signifying humannesses: the onça, a spotted panther whose bite goes straight to the brain. But no, for the Frenchman driving through it in his car, the tropical forest is a world of objects, an uninhabited nature. If for him it belongs to a 'different order' than our own forest, the fruit of the careful labour of signifying humans, the very same humans who continually chatter about the panacea of care, this can only be because it exists without us; the fight of a Black Brazilian with a panther, through which a Parisian painter can communicate with an entire people, is just an illusion which must be scrubbed out of the picture. The minerality of the rainforest, its metallic hardness, its bony perseverance, are those of nature without the human, nature absolutely uninhabited by any humanity, whether that of humans or that of the plants and beasts to which the rite introduces humans. Nature in itself. The inescapable presupposition of all science, so they say. The same thing that a contemporary Cartesian philosopher, meditating before his stove on the corner of rue d'Ulm and rue Gay-Lussac, perched on his comfy banquette in a Parisian bistro, represents to himself by subtracting himself from the 'world for us' in which he lives cushioned by care and attention: a purely objective ancestral world, datable in the billions of years, anterior to the appearance of the human species, that is to say, as he understands it, anterior to the appearance of sensibility—as if there were no sensibility other than that of the learned human species and, above all, as if humanity itself were a single species. A curious sort of realism, this: a realism without experience and without magic, one which destroys all encounters and all transcendence in advance, and which, in fact, shares with the most absolute idealisms the illusion of having triumphed over finitude, over actual life and death—over the jaguar and negritude, over the death that gets you in its jaws and eats you up. All of which is quite typical of the melancholy of the European metaphysician, who, unable to withstand the shock, the clash of sensation, the manifestation that summons one to existence at the same time as it annihilates, does everything he can to avoid having to endure it. Memory of a Hegelian friend sitting opposite me in a café, sated by the scent of a freshly opened pack of Marlboros from which he will not smoke a single cigarette, drunk on seeing me sip from a glass of wine he will not touch. The realist, like the idealist, doesn't really smoke or drink. That the first shock of the tropics, for the great French Amerindianist, should be an impression of uninhabited nature, without man and without predator, is scarcely to be believed. How is it possible for one to set foot upon the land of the New World only to apprehend it primarily under the auspices of pre-subjective ancestrality, of naked objectivity? Pure speculation. A purely speculative realism, straight out of a Parisian bistro. After Santos and the forest, Lévi-Strauss arrives in São Paulo, where he frequents another exotic flora, that of the gran fino, the city's intellectual and political elite. A fortuitously mimetic flora made up of individuals who, like the Congolese in Hergé's *Tintin in the Congo*, each take on the attributes of a function (a god?) of European society: the liberal, the communist, the surrealist poet, the painter, the musicologist.... Another way of confessing the Bantu negritude of White Brazilians, unbearable to the scholar and from which, in his eyes, only a few individual success stories—cariocas by birth or by vocation—are excepted: the doctors Oswaldo Cruz and Carlos Chagas, the writer Euclides da Cunha and the musician Heitor Villa-Lobos, who both drew their inspiration from the warlike musical trance of the Nordeste: Candomblé hymns, the languid, battle-hardened rhythms of copoeira, the foliões carnival party crowds led by Yoruba groups sowing debauchery and public disorder, and later, the violent blocos de indios, banned but resurrected by the Sons of Gandhi, African India subverting the colonial invention of a West Indian Africa, Olodum, rhythmic quilombo, the polkas and mazurkas combined with Nordeste rhythms, xaxado, baiãos, côco, pernambuco frevo, virginal Midsummer processions, pifano bandas mimicking the jaguar dance, forrô accordionists.... An arid land, the end of the world, you will agree, not under-populated but 'populated' like the neither tragic nor uninhabited desert of Franny Deleuze's dream, which is 'only a desert because of its ochre colour and its blazing, shadowless sun', and certainly not because of an absence of humanity or animality. Not deserted by way of the subtraction of human beings and therefore identical to a pure world of objects (the only notion of the desert available to someone meditating by their stove in a cold country), a desert teeming with multiplicitous, turbulent crowds. Not the crowds of Calcutta to which Lévi-Strauss, curiously, devotes a chapter in *Tristes Tropiques*, crowds of degraded beggars bathing in their own filth (always this fascinated disgust for excrement), but joyful, predatory packs—Spinozan packs, or rather Espinosian, Luso-Indo-African, adorned with balangandas, feathers, and necklaces made of animal teeth, wearing oriental turbans: the (ethnically, musically) anthropophagous cannibal crowds of the Nordeste carnival in the face of which European logic, morality, and religion suddenly and inexplicably falter. The journey is indeed intensive. You can't just drive, ride a donkey, or walk across the interior to get there. First of all because this desert cannot be crossed, it is only really accessible from the periphery, from the mobile edge, affected by the permanent emotions of groups, gangs, blocos, and is never the object of an internal conquest. And secondly because if you're too French, too sedentary in one way or another, you can just leave it to your wife, if she's an Americanist and a good schizo dreamer. But just as he erases the primitive scene of the devouring of one creature by another from the rainforest, Lévi-Strauss erases his Americanist wife, his Franny, his Dinamene, from the narrative. Dina Dreyfus, who nonetheless was there with him on the trip, in São Paulo, at his side among the Bororo and Nambikwara Indians. Dina, the missing woman of *Saudades do Brasil*, who was never seen in a single photograph, and who never took a single photograph. Moreover, in order for one to confuse *saudade* with a feeling of inexplicable lack, with sad nostalgia for a bygone era, in order to confuse the excessive presence of tropical beings with that of objects, the woman *must* disappear—in 1938, and after. It is necessary to ignore what only a woman cannot fail to make evident: that *saudade* is said precisely of the excessive presence, now, of those with whom one is, there, at this moment, well, happy, blessed to be with them, yet separated from them, so inaccessible. To ignore the fact that *saudade* refers precisely to that uniquely American feeling of the violent, almost vertiginous happiness that accompanies the schizo dreamer's position on the edge of the crowd. Dina could have told Claude this. She who used to hang out with Mário de Andrade, author of *Macunaíma*, the novel of Afro-Indigenous anthropophagy that founded Brazilian modernismo. Dina, who, together with Mário, created the first Brazilian ethnological society, and through whom Claude met the author of *Pau-Brasil*—the other great modernist figure, inseparable from Mário, from whom tropicalism, Cinema Novo, and post-Levi-Straussian Brazilian anthropology would soon be born: Oswald de Andrade. The complex rhizome of Eduardo Viveiros de Castro's *Cannibal Metaphysics*: aberrant theoretical alliances, indigenous and Euro-American, and at the very bottom of the large sheet of paper where he sketches the rhizome, ringed in black felt tip pen, clearly set apart from all the names of more or less eccentric conceptmongers—Gilles, Félix, Claude, Bruno, Roy, etc.—the name Oswald; the name of Eduardo's Rhizome. Now, what Oswald said about the discovery of Brazil, about the first shock of the tropics, is that 'before the Portuguese discovered Brazil, Brazil had discovered happiness'. The most incomprehensible of things for those who can only think of absolute anteriority by subtracting everything that is—a woman, a Black man wrestling with a jaguar—or, like Descartes, by subtracting all the sense data which, up until now, he has accepted as the most true and certain thing in the world: that he is here, sitting by the stove, wearing a dressing gown, with this paper in his hands, etc. Unable to conceive of anything that may have existed before he discovered it, saw it, thought it, and wanted it, other than as a primitive existence—and unable to conceive of this primitive existence as anything other than an impersonal world, ridiculously impoverished and insentient, crystallised into pure, measurable, and dateable objects. A storehouse of raw materials. But before the Old World brought in whole caravels of canned, subtractable, and transportable consciousness, the New World was already an entirely unprecedented invention. Not a primitive happiness which, like Jean-Jacques Rousseau's semi-wild, neolithic paradise, could be attributed to the scarcity of isolated men on an island lost between nature and culture, a fragile moment of happiness on the road to unhappiness. No, not a single happiness, but many: the happiness of a world of people, made up only of people, of multiple humanities, vegetal, animal, and mineral, an entirely human nativity or primitiveness, full of plants, birds, trees, and rivers, stones, and hunter-fishermen, all human, as in the Indian origin stories: more or less transformed, but equally human. A world-society, a 'world-map' as Oswald calls it, across which are traced the wander lines via which humanity transforms and recreates itself, passing from one species to another. Not a happiness relative to a better or a worse, but precisely that simply lived beatitude toward which must strive, as best he can, the untransformed man of the temperate regions, those regions to which Bento de Espinosa, the Amsterdam Pernambucan, introduces the idea: the Tupi idea of a feminine sun, a feminine unity, a loving goddess, Guaraci or the absolutely infinite Substance, from which each is born in proportion to their ability to love all things, whatever their rank in the speculative scale of beings, as so many unique persons, inimitable essences, and to love themselves, to enjoy themselves through this insatiable and joyful alteration of themselves by all that is not their own. Obviously, only a woman can know this. Or a man who wants to be a woman. No wonder that Deleuze, faithful to Franny, hallucinates Spinoza as a resurrected Heliogabalus. Artaud's Heliogabalus, the crowned anarchist, the solar king dressed as a woman. In which case, to understand what the reign of Guaraci implies and what it excludes, and to propose it as a new ethics to the men of the meridian, one must somehow communicate with such royalty. But having come to participate in the foundation of the University of São Paulo, Lévi-Strauss is a French colonist who is fundamentally catechetical, a socialist missionary sensitive above all to the progress of tropical medicine and the intellectual education of children. A man of discipline. He knew nothing, or pretended to know nothing, of what Brazil had discovered before the Portuguese discovered Brazil, or of what the Portuguese in turn discovered when they became Brazilian. Namely, according to Oswald: a communism and a surrealism that are immediately palpable, in life itself, not pre-formed in any idea, neither imported nor exportable, in the face of which the communist idea and the surrealist idea, since they are just ideas, simply crumble. A communism and a surrealism that are not speculative but eminently affective since, according to Oswald, Brazilians have never engaged in speculation, that Latin art of control, of looking down upon and spying on things. A communism that is neither urban nor suburban, neither border nor continental, without an International and yet planetary, identical to Pindorama, the world-society-planet Brazil which includes the roteiros, chaotic migratory routes and popular scenarios of the sertão, northeastern cordels; and a polyglot, illiterate surrealism. A divinatory communism and surrealism, a world of hallucinatory visões, in the foothills of which the objectified ideas of Franco-Batavian European science drop dead, and the hypotheses with which the German masters indulge themselves evaporate into thin air—all of that I-cosmos or cosmos-me, I-is-everything or All-is-me, I-All or All-Me, All-All or I-Me, I-Me-Thou or You-Me-Thou, I-Me-Thou or You-Me-Thou. All that hogwash. Is the carnivalesque surrealist poet, the 'surrealist poet' function of the gran fino paulista, of which Claude speaks in *Tristes Tropiques*, really Oswald de Andrade? The unspeakable Oswald who debauched his young female students, and in whose company Claude visited the Iguazu Falls? Who else? Of course it was the great Oswald!—not some bourgeois Paulist infatuated with the Parisian avant-garde. It's true that Oswald invented Brazil, in the early 1920s, in Place Clichy, and that it owes more to the friendship of a Swiss poet than to his frequentation of the Tupi. Oswald de Andrade, a species from the temperate regions transplanted into a tropical environment, a unique

sample artificially maintained and put on display like a Parisian nov-
elty in a provincial shop window; a Frenchman who is seriously French,
that is to say seriously aware of his language, or, what amounts to
the same thing, a Frenchman who was an enthusiastic reader of Céline
in '32, how can he claim three years later, when he arrives in Brazil, to
be unaware of what Place Clichy is capable of, what it can do in terms
of escape and voyages...and the denunciation of colonial imbecility?
The great flight, as far away as possible, to the ends of the earth,
across vast geographical and historical spaces beyond the oceans
and continents, and, at the same time, the retreat into the intimate
and sinuous depths, as-yet unexplored, of the language and thought
of his own people. Never one without the other. To see in Oswald only
a Mardi Gras surrealist, just as ancient historians saw Heliogabalus
as nothing more than an idiot dressed as a king, is to fail to appreci-
ate Oswald's 'We were never catechized. We made Carnival instead'—
the Carnival that the Portuguese caravels could not have imported
because, like communism and surrealism, like Christ, born in Bahia
or Belém in Para, it was already there, already made by Brazil before
Brazil was even discovered. 'We made Carnival instead. The Indian
dressed up as senator of the Empire, aping Pitt.' This is the persistent
image, the carnival image that becomes more vivid as the attention
wanders, the concretistic-anti-speculative image par excellence, the
antidote to those ideas that want to govern everything and condemn
to death all those who do not know how to submit to them, and it is
also the hallucinatory image of Bento of Amsterdam: 'The Indian
dressed up as senator of the Empire', Felipe Camarão. But also Vir-
gulino Ferreira da Silva, King of the Cangaço, dressed in wrought and
studded leather, decorated with coins and Hebrew characters, whose
royal headdress Claude may well have admired when, in July 1938, it
was put on display for the public in Santana de Ipanema alongside
da Silva's severed head. For no matter what the king's melanin, white,
black, copper, or brown skinned, he is always an Indian. Because of
the curious anteriority of Carnival, of the Brazilian and his disguise,
to the discovery of Brazil. Bento-the-Portuguese, for whom a 'scabby
black Brazilian' is the same thing as an 'Ethiopian', knows this very

well: it was an African emperor, the Niguse Negest of Ethiopia, heir to the kings of Aksum, custodian of a literally aboriginal, pre-Roman Christianity, to whom Pêro da Covilha, at the end of the fifteenth century, having left Portugal for the Indies to seek the mythical kingdom of Priest John, the primitive Christian land irrigated by a river of precious stones flowing directly from Paradise, handed over a proposal for alliance written in the hand of the King of Portugal. Brazilian or Ethiopian, Indigenous or African, Felipe Camarão or Henrique Dias, it makes no difference, it's the same Indian royalty, from those Indies that the Portuguese discovered while searching for India, the same undatable figure of an aboriginal royalty in Emperor's costume, through which something circulates between the Roman, the Greco-Mediterranean, and the Indian and, passing between them and under them, undoes and denatures them, making them something else—not something that results from them, their exposed contradiction or their synthesis or syncretic unity, but something anterior to both, something already made before they split off from one another: not their primitive natural unity—yet another idea haunted by the anxiety of degeneration so characteristic of the melancholic psyche—but their primary fabricated unity, entirely fabricated, fabricated from scratch. This is what making Carnival is all about: stitching together the Primitive by sewing an Emperor's robe onto an Indian skin. And here lies the anteriority of Carnival to the discovery of Brazil: the anteriority of this stitching, this fabrication. Nothing could be more astonishing, more astounding, for a Mediterranean, a Greco-Latin, used to fabricating systems of ideas based on the only emotion of which he is perhaps still capable: surprise at the impossible. For the Brazilian invention is not made for him at all: the panic-stricken perplexity that seized him left him on the sidelines for good, logically powerless, discouraged from taking the slightest idea out of his transatlantic baggage or trying to form any new ones. To land on the coast of the New World, provided you really do change tack and land, is to discover this invention, to be struck by it, to be transfixed by happiness. But to discover it is to become it. It is to tip over into this improbable anteriority. To arrive as if returning. *Going native*. For the swallowing of

36

Bishop Sardinha by the Caeté is already Oswald de Andrade. What did it really consist in, the colonial catastrophe, the clash of the tropics? Not that the Portuguese was eaten by the Indian, but that he himself became a devourer of Portuguese, Dutch, French, Italians, Poles, Japanese, Ukrainians, of all the fugitives of a civilisation that Brazil continually eats up—and also of Indians. To have been invited to the Tupi smokehouse and to have felt so comfortable there, so fond of the skilfully smoked foreign flesh, that he ended up hearing in the indigenous din the festive, sonorous dimension of Carnival. Of course, there will always be fugitives unable to flee that far, moralists unable to understand that from Salvador's Embaxaida Africana, the Black Rome, to Heitor's Bachianas brasileiras, from the Putaria of baile funk to Caetano Veloso's funk melodico, the same anthropophagic principle prevails: the same barbarism, violent or gentle, indecent or tender, more or less intellectualised but always exclusively affective, the same hunger, sexual and anthropophagic—since Brazil, after also devouring Freud, was done with the bourgeois moral drama of frustration and sublimation, and unabashedly revelled in the sexual act like a jaguar in the fresh blood of its prey. Heitor Villa-Lobos: Bach eaten by the Nordeste. Caetano Veloso, the tropicalist: Godard's cinema, Morin's sociology and even Lévi-Strauss's anthropology, eaten up by the Bahian Reconcavo. No influence, no relationship of filiation. Nothing that has anything to do with that sacrosanct recognition in which Europeans are so lacking but through which they interpret all the alienation, all the poverty, and all the hollow cavities they have managed to carve out in their own existence and in that of others. Or rather, only that paradoxical recognition which Bergson referred to as false recognition, but which has nothing false about it: the impression of *déjà vécu*—of something already lived—that comes from the momentary lapsing of our attention from what life normally requires for the preservation of our species, qua species separated from the rest of the living world. Namely, in essence: subjecting the world to our industry and taking part in the merciless slaughter of everything that is not us. A brief moment of inattention that detaches a fantastic double from our present perception in the form of a resistant image, unrelated to what memory is capable of remembering, an undatable image of the present which makes it seem as if it has always been there: because it has always been there. The newest, the most surprising of visions is thus properly re-recognised, and all the more so because it resembles nothing recognisable. This world of primitive and timeless visions in which children and adventurers live because they are so open to seeing things they have never seen before. And the anteriority of Brazil is the same. Arriving as if returning: the New World so new that it emerges from the ocean like *déjà vu*—like a world from which one had strayed only to find it again after centuries of absence. The colonial flight of the West toward a *terra incognita* repeats in reverse the very old, indeed truly ancestral, flight of the first men, aborigines exhausted by the incessant noise of the World Forest populated by a proliferating, fermenting vegetation, to say nothing of the animals. A forest where even the smallest tree, populated by epiphytes swarming with other species, exhibits a profusion of branches and stems, leaves, flowers, and fruits, of tangled shapes and colours that are all human presences. The flight of these indigenous ancestors who left the world, lost the world, only to reach a land untouched by humanity on the other side of the ocean. Fleeing the forest, where one only ever enters in single file, according to a contingent order that must be strictly repeated on the way back, and returning in boatloads, in total disorder, ever more numerous, but never succeeding in dominating the immensity of the sertão-world by sheer numbers. In short: more aborigine than ever, already an aborigine, the Portuguese colonist, Latinised like all the fugitives come from the Old World, was already there where he first set foot, on this quay, this mobile edge of the people-world where he landed. It was there that his attention finally wandered away for good, and everything he had brought with him, from all eras, philosophy, music, science, French, German, Batavian, Jewish, Catholic or Protestant, Western, Eastern or African, all of it—Jesus, the Negus, Priest John— was already there, along with all the characters in Oswald's thesis, rejected by the University of São Paulo and duly Frenchified, all the names in History (*in ordo ordinans*): Homer, Kojève, Kelsen, Engels,

Frazer, the insomniac priests of Lake Nemi, Peter, Paul and the Martyr Fathers, Constantine, Attila and Genseric, Francis of Assisi, Savonarola, the monk Martin Luther, Aristotle, Lazarus, Matthew, Mark and Luke, Paracelsus, Homo Sapiens, the bird-man, all the beings of the funambulistic Macaque Kingdom along with their leader Macaque Saru from whom the Japanese descend through cross-breeding with a Chinese princess, Cicero, Fustel de Coulange, Virgil, Tucidide, Solon, Caesar, Zarathustra, Michelangelo, Bachofen. All of them were already there, as were Bach, Godard, Morin, and Lévi-Strauss, those same aborigines who left naked and returned to America in Latin clothes. And their existence, every one of them, owes in reality to their undatable presence in their Brazilian double. Heitor was never influenced by Bach, nor by the music of the Nordeste, where he disappeared for eight years, scrubbed out from the virgin world of cultural institutions: Johann Sebastian Bach and the Mothers of the Candomblé saints have always been in Brazil, from the very first quay; they were born there, and are reborn there every time a fugitive is devoured by an Indian or an Indian dresses up in the costume of an Emperor.

Heliogabalus

Of course Bento had never seen him before, his scabby black Rasta-
farian Brazilian, his Pernambucan Negusa Nagast. Who's ever seen
anything like that? A Black Indo-Eastern army equipped with throwing weapons, driving away the masters of the Dutch anomaly, masters
at the cutting edge of commercial, political, and military progress
from the West Indies. Points versus cutting edge. American anomaly
versus European anomaly—or, more precisely, versus what the man
dressed as Oswald, the European *homo habitus*, is able to understand
as an anomaly by way of his chronic messianism, which prevents him
from thinking of the anomalous as anything other than a vague pre-
figuration of something that is never going to happen. An invisible
moose that cannot be shot with an arrow. And of course it's a question of the double. But not the one we think, the double of the Hoff-
mannian-Freudian tale of castration anxiety or the Dostoyevskian
double, Goliadkin the younger versus Goliadkin the elder, doubles
from cold countries where it's still a question of father and son. That's
Peter Balling's story, the father's auditory hallucination of the son.
Filiation and hereditary reproduction, communication between humans
of the same species, loving one another and keeping themselves in
the same state as much as possible, without undergoing any transformations, without taking tightrope walks toward bird people, fish
people, Buriti people, and even water people: Preto, Verde, Pacari,

Ponte, São Pedro and Santa Catarina—in short, without making a people. Daddy's boy. A patriarchy whose form is daddy-mommy-child, jiji-cricri nailed up on the triangular essence of the Father. No. The story of Bento, the visual hallucination, the strict, feminine identity of seeing and the seen, as only a woman, Clarice Lispector, or a man dressed as a woman, can still understand it, the story of Bento, of the first Brazilian Bento, before Bento Prado Jr. and Bento Nunes, those readers of Clarice and Oswald—this story is indeed American and Indian. What happens when, in Mexico or Brazil, daddy-mommy no longer fucks the Innate pederast: the kid Artaud, 'soot of grandma's ass, much more than of father-mother's', or Heliogabalus, son of his uncle, and, above all (and, all things considered, exclusively) of all the Julias, all primo-generators, Julia Domna, Moesa, Soemia and Mamoea, mothers, aunts and sisters, who, definitively blurring filiation, the idiotic father-mother journey and the child in which begetting is locked up, together give birth to the pederast king in a cradle of sperm. The barbarian matriarchy replaces family histories and the Oedipo-Christian orgy with symbioses and transversal connections between heterogeneous peoples. Julia, Domna and the others play a part in all of this: the earth which is living in Syria, where there are stones which are alive and where, through ritual channels, the blood of man joins the plasma of animals. An anarchy whose own logic, already inapplicable to the Roman world, induces panic in the European scholar, who, like Claudius, can only see similarities between one country and another, can only travel from one country to another within the same Roman, logically Roman, Empire. A barbaric metaphysical order that makes the Syrian aborigine communicate everywhere and at all times with the Indian aborigine, the marrano and the maroon, the schizo, the philosopher, and the Emperor, all of whom are in contact with Latin. Bento de Espinosa and Benedictus Spinoza, Heliogabalus and Marcus Aurelius Antoninus, Potiguaçu and Camarão: all those who have a double name. The first name refers to a non-Latin people, and therefore to a multiplicity of peoples, thirty peoples from the East or the West, from the peninsula or basin, shores or plateaus, revolving in an incessant migratory trance around each first name—for the first name, whether Iberian, Syrian or Potiguara, is never the name of one person but of all persons. And then a second name, Latin, as a unique person in Universal History—this second name is also not their own, but in a different sense. A double de-personality under the joint effect of the diastolic multiplication of the first name and the systolic tightening of the second. An Indian dressed as an Emperor: at once drawn out of himself, far from himself, by the crowd of peoples moving on the surface of the Earth, and retreating to the very edge of the crowd. Both at once. Always the same schizo-American Carnival position. Bento's hallucination, an image of the double? Yes. But not the wretched, nasty little double—you know, the one that doubles up on everyone's little self, tucked away in all the dark corners of Oedipal children's bedrooms, between their mothers' thighs, in the evil eye of the father and even in the mirrors of the house. No, Bento's hallucination is an image of the Great Double, the Duplicitous, which has nothing to do with how you imagine the Other sees you or doesn't: a self fleeing extensively along lines of migration, across the kingdom of the species, but also concentrated into a point of royal exception, above all living beings. All the more exceptional because it flees with the crowd, all the more crowded because it stands out from the crowd. This is the other himself that Bento sees at the foot of his bed. His own duplicity. Spinoza *als* Spinoza, as the Germans say. Bento doing a Spinoza. Terrific theatre! What's this? Spinoza, a pederast king dressed as a woman, a Carnival Emperor? A scabby black Brazilian who has had done with Mama's vagina and the prostitutes' slits, to be born instead directly from Grandmother's arsehole; 'soot' shat out by Substance-Nature? Get it? And the new Espinosian cogito: cogito ego-soot. Some kind of gag? Not at all. Nothing could more serious. A matter of sperm, blood, and shit. Free of all disgust. Afro-Polish Brazilian Leminski the concretist knows nothing of disgust, does not confuse a hole with the absence of God like you do, because nothing is better than a *bela cagada*, a beautiful shit, a beautiful scattering of shit, and no shit can compare to that of the Beloved...the true gold of Brazil. A non-Christian nativity through the ass, anal genesis of the pederast by the feminine, without any need to complicate everything with stories about a carpenter cucked by an angel. Born, like Helioga-balus, in a cradle of Iberian, Jewish, and Arab sperm, Bento, under the name of Benedictus, like Heliogabalus, enters into the Roman Empire 'from behind'. Like Heliogabalus, he practised a systematic insurrec-tion, *more geometrico* (that's where you do it from behind) against the division between Roman and barbaric, order and anarchy, con-sonance and aberration, and like him, he transformed the most unre-servedly barbaric expenditure and the most absolute disorder into an experience of the most perfect and joyous unity. And vice versa. No offence, but you'll definitely have a hard time understanding this, you who think you are Greeks, marching in goose-step toward the spiritual salvation of the West while grumbling about how animals are poor in world. You need to be a bit of a sorcerer, a bit of a shaman, to know that Spinoza is American, Ethiopian, and therefore Syrian, that his thought, like that of the thousand plateaus, has to do with indigenous thought. The voyage is intensive, it's true. But it does happen. For real. And while Lévi-Strauss never really landed in Gua-nabara Bay, where the Corcovado and the Sugarloaf Peak seemed to him, as Caetano sings, like the stumps of missing teeth in the four corners of a toothless mouth, Deleuze really did land in Franny's dream, on the warm ochre earth of her dream, in the desolate bay of the Gallo-Roman plateau of Millevaches, an empty space, *melo vacua*, the Highlands, the Limousin sertão, a veritable sea of undulating hills, already fulfilling—elsewhere and in the very place where it must always be fulfilled, in the same place—the prophecy, which applies to all sertaõs, of becoming-sea, and for all seas, upon approaching their coast, of becoming-sertão, surrounded by herds of granite blocks, a sierra of Occitan cows frozen in stone, and also and above all, a Celtic planalto where a thousand rivers find their source, flowing into the Dordogne in the direction of the colonial slave-trading Atlantic Ocean, and into the Loire, the royal river. A sea and a bay-world-cha-pada, where a thousand peoples and civilisations are constantly intermingling, and where Gilles feels at ease, far upstream of the estuaries and valleys where white power shops out its molarising machines. A Brazil within France. And don't tell me that a plateau isn't a bay, that the hinterland isn't a sea. How else are you supposed to land a country? Always the sanctimonious tone of the shopkeepers of privileges, merchants of sugar and slaves. In Rio as in Limousin, the same jagged mouth of irregular granite blocks and crystalline peaks that devours you. And do we even know what stone is? What stone does to people? Another piece of Pernambucan wisdom. Educated 'by stone', as Joao Cabral de Melo Neto says—by lessons, in other words—to learn its impersonal, non-emphatic diction from the outside in, to get it into your head through dictations, moral recitations, poetics and orthodontics. The French academician, the child of the Communale, does not like toothless mouths. He undoubtedly prefers the regular and complete dentition proper to scientific phonation. Yet in the sertão, in the Brazilian bay-plateau, another kind of education happens, another education by stone. From inside to outside and before school even starts. There, stone does not know how to teach, how to give lessons, and would not learn anything if it did try to teach. There, the stone is inside from birth; the kernel or the almond of that petrified tree which is the sertanejo. Even as far as Guanabara, where it takes the form of a hunchback and two brothers and, in Gavea, a king of Tyr which, for real, welcomed Claude to Rio. And since it can't be taught, you can't explain it: just look at the teeth of Nordeste kids spoilt by hunger and sugar, and how Glauber proudly displays them between his own jaws. Because from inside to outside, it is only in stone that the man of the sertão can express himself: in a stone idiom, in stony words that would tear up his mouth if he did not coat each one of them in the sugar of a smooth-sweet intonation, if he did not take the care to candy them one by one, which takes time, so that he speaks slowly and reluctantly...thus rotting his teeth a little more, reducing a block of granite to a stump by coating it again and again in sugar. And so they speak an increasingly rare language with an increasingly toothless mouth. Total incompatibility between the orthodontic language of the Parisian Écoles and the language of the Plateaus. It's going to be hard to speak about all this without talking in a decayed language. All the more decayed because it will be coated to make bearable the pain of the stone, which rises from within and, as João Cabral says, comes to afflict the skin with 'a dull and dirty black'. The dull, dirty bereaved skin of the pau mulatto, in permanent moult, beneath which emerge, in wide strips of flesh, the soft, warm ochre of the earth, almost orange, and the vivid green and red of the tourmaline...which Claude could not fail to see. Because the scabby black Brazilian, mulatto, a man without colour, is also a man of colour, the achromatic man a chromatic tree. That is what 'mulatto' means. Untinted *and* tanned with all the hues of the tropics. Black *and* tawny. Hard crystals of granite *and* melting crystals of sugar. Can you see him now? This Black who insists on sitting by Espinosa's bedside: glittering with a thousand unstable colours, proudly opening his tooth-less cannibal mouth to respond to your astonishment with a few care-fully chosen sweet words, dressed in the costume of an Emperor? Are you such a stranger to Bento d'Espinosa or Spinoza that you don't see yourself in such an image? In this Brazilian image of yourself? Do you still need it to be explained further?

Cartesio

I know, my dear Bento. You don't believe me. You don't believe that Spinoza went to Brazil. A beautiful lie. A big lizard-tongue lie. And, as Clarice says, writing's 'not worth a damn'. So what about the spinozo-marxo-heideggerian-hegelianism of the philosophers, the little monster of the classrooms? A tiny spinosaurus, a spinozasaurus, stupid, inoffensive, but still surly, inevitably, at being so inoffensive and so paltry. A little anomal.... Well, yes he did. He did go there. This was confirmed by the Museu Nacional do Brasil. An establishment specialising in spiked, plated, horned, crested, and feathered lizards. The proof? The meticulously detailed account is officially recorded, in the first person, by Paulo Leminski *fils* (a professor of History and Writing) in *Catatau*. I got this personally from a friend at the Parc de Belle Vue. And all the rest. So, since we have some explaining to do, let's dot the *i*s and cross the *t*s. 'Catatau', *n.m.*: the sound of a crashing fall, a collapse. In Portugal: a beating, or a penis. A wank and a dick. In Brazil: a big thing or a little thing. In Bahia, something ugly. A big or small spinosaurus, very ugly. Black and scabby? Or a buzzing discussion, a swarm of polyglot, glossolalic, onomatopoietic words, names, and phrases. A giant or a dwarf, a Brazilian lizard, there on the asphalt, living there for millions of years before you or I arrived. Ten thousand surviving species. Long before you and long after. The extinction of the spinosaurs? That's the real fib, the real lizard-lie!

Ten thousand bem-te-vi, ten thousand little Tyrannides, tiny and terrifying, who have always already seen you, capable of catching and killing a hawk, frying a kraut. How do you think it would have been possible to produce, here at home, in the under-equipped laboratories of our white universities, little scabby black saurians, miniature monsters like a German Spinoza, a Marrano Berber phenomenologist, a communist or whatever, without this colossal fall of Catatau, of Spinoza in America? But, you'll say, because you're bound to have found out by now: *Catatau* is the story of Descartes going to Brazil, not Spinoza. Yes, and who else is going to take the beating? Isn't Spinoza Descartes's catatau? His ejaculatory organ? His poetic, auto-poetic power? Even the Academy has trouble hiding that fact. Every time it tries to explain Descartes without Spinoza, it just comes out with some hackneyed nonsense. Why shouldn't Descartes get beaten off in the first person? And isn't 'Spinoza' the name of Descartes taking a beating? In short: Bento's hallucination is also Descartes in the tropics, the toothless smile of Cartesio. Bento Cartesio!

Here you are like the dog without feathers, the voiceless tree of João Cabral, eaten away to the point of lack. Deprived of what you think you do not lack—because you don't have it, because you never had it. Yet without it you are lost, as a needle is not lost, as a mirror is not broken. Lost, having fallen short of the human. Your human thread snapped. Believe it. And, like Cartesio de Catatau, taken on board at Nassau along with Wagener, Post, Golijath, and Eckhout to make an inventory of the colonial possessions of New Holland, plants, animals, and men (always this shopkeeper's logic), astonished and delighted by Brazil, you still expect explanations: someone to repeat the sentence you have just read to you in another form to authenticate and clarify it and prevent any misinterpretation, over and over again but without emphasis, without changing its meaning one iota, only to find yourself, quite intact, in this logical continuity of the redundant lesson, without having lost a single feather in the process, still bearing the same name, just one name, yours and certainly not that of a stranger whom, what's worse, you have never even seen before in your life, the name of a stranger in which you can sense it swarming with ten thousand bird names, ten thousand feather headdresses, ten thousand ornaments for a featherless dog. So: let Descartes be Descartes, Spinoza Spinoza, Hegel Hegel, Artaud Artaud, Camarão Camarão, Lampiao Lampiao, Moreira Moreira, and, dear Bento, above all, let nobody be called Bento: A = A. In short, let it never become a totem, never let a mask be attached to your proper name, the mask of another humanity: guaraní-kaiowá, munduruku, kadiwéu, arapiuns, pankará, xocó, tapuio, xeréu, yanomami, asuriní, cinta larga, kayapó, waimiri atroari, tariana, pataxó. And conversely, never let your proper name become a mask for an Indian, a Carnival costume. You expect explanations, and, like Cartesio, all you get is information that is always new and always irrelevant, and you never know from one sentence to the next, from one word to the next, what to expect. You are ready to throw in the towel, to withdraw from this incessant abortion of continuity, this permanent frustration of your expectations, and stop reading. And then, dear Bento, what is it with calling you Bento, calling you all these bird names? So as to deprive you of your family name, your spiritual family name, your great spiritual family, to stop talking to you with our backs to the river, hatching the great eggs of our common prose with you, backs to the river—to stop talking to you, my featherless dog, back turned on you. To settle down on the quayside, on the edge of the river, on the edge of its living matter, its thick and muddy blood, to drag yourself along featherless, unable to brood anymore, among what lives, stripped of all your clothes from the cold country, down to the light shirt of a sunburned man, right down to the cloud clothes you dream of making for yourself. To expose yourself to the turmoil, to the painful clashes proper to a life in which a thousand lives swarm. To this submerging density of reality from which the great Enochian families of thought protect themselves, the heautontimoroumenotic families who apply a learned, methodical, and laborious torture, with their backs to living peoples, in order to keep their own name and repel the attacks of zoopsia to which they are nonetheless constantly subject, as they hallucinate repugnant saurians. Who, in order to counter the fixed ideas that, like a scabby black Brazilian, constantly assail them, learn the language of the angels, only to touch with the tip of a transcendental reduction or a speculative calculation—head back, lips to the sky but closed, from as far away as one can imagine—the thing itself, the foul beast wallowing in the thick mud of the featherless river. To settle there on the edge of the quays, on the repulsive inner wall of the decayed mouth of Guanabara, facing Niteroi, rua Acre, which bears the name of another border, of other foothills: the Andean acres of the undiscovered Kaxinawa indigenous land in the Amazon, a tropical, flower-filled Palestine where the men, seringueiros, take their name from a plant, and where once floated, as on the quays of the port of Rio, the plague-like stench of smoked rubber and fossil fuels, where jagunços continue to assassinate insurgent kings of the sertão-forest, Chico Mendes, lookalike of the pacifist President of Eldorado overthrown on the roofs of the mansion at the Parque Lague, at the foot of the Corcovado, another Carioca tooth stump, in Glauber's *Entranced Earth*, ally of a kayapo-metutkire Indian chief with a lip plate, labial ambassador of the Forest-people. You, rua Acre, with the silly young Nordestine from *The Hour of the Star*, Clarice's biblical Nordestine, as stupid, frail, and wretched as she, of a poverty so filthy that no friend of man will go there to see if he is still well-off enough to eat his fill and babble vague thoughts of revolt. Except Clarice, who is forced to put on a man's skin to dress as a woman. Tortured like her by hunger, suffocated by a chronic cough, head under a thin pillow and anonymous and mediocre enough to be delighted, like her, vile creature, by the crowing of a rooster out of nowhere in the bloody dawn, coming to your bed from the quays of the port. You, who became this woman, dear Bento. Not Marilyn, the all-pink one, but this Macabéa of Clarice, grey with grime, as resistant to the progress of man as a thousand-year-old insect, as a pious Jewess who no Greek would make eat pork. You, called a liar by your boyfriend for telling him the only truth you know: that a cock crows in your street...to your unhappy boyfriend, an Olympic thinker, a learned diplomat, a brilliant opportunist ready to steal your best friend because she is, admit it, far more suitable than you for his future career as a parliamentary deputy. But you too, from that grey, mulatto negritude of the rua Acre, you now hear the cock crowing. And you see it.

You see the bloody dawn and the bird, where there are no animals. Feathered moose. Evident in its invisibility. Where the waters freeze, thick and stagnant, in front of the vast warehouses leaking behind the unspeakable bridge thrown across the bay to Niteroi, doors without doors, a malodorous gaping hole. Something, says João Cabral, like the stagnation of dirty locked-up life in the hospital or the asylum. Visible only to a lizard's eye...detached from the body, memoryless; since sight is immediately the sight of what has always been present, for millennia, before Christ, and in the most distant future, after Christ. This curious combination of mediocrity and brilliance.... Of insignificance and infinity.... Rosemonde the Salamander. The girl in the film? I say Rosemonde to try to explain, my dear Bento. Because we, this curious combination of woman and rival animal, are not roses, neither Marilyn nor Rosemonde/Bulle, too impertinent, too pungent, and too beautiful, born in the mind of a Swiss documentary filmmaker specialising in economics...more like Rosetta-Salamander in the muddy water of the river, the cold soil of the woods. An ugly little proletarian.... Filmed without sentiment. A white-skinned Belgian negro, pink from the cold. Rosetta de Espinosa! We'll never make it any other way. Right? We'll never make it to life without it. We'll never get back to life without it. You can write ten thousand pages about the *vie sauvage* in the sun of Haute-Provence, surrounded by the scent of lavender, but it won't do any good! You have to be a different kind of Belgian, a different kind of northerner, a different kind of smoker! It's true, it's true! But how do you tell them? With their reductions, they'll never get anything but a more concentrated, more flavoursome base, just enough to excite their satiated bodies to have yet another meal, as desperately assured as it is copious.... Drizzled with bottled wine pumped full of sulphites to save them from this grey rot, the microbial flora, the scum, the millions of live bugs that frighten the pants off them.... A coq au vin bourguignon for dinner! To impress their latest gf, good deputy of things and men...necessarily conservative. Reassuring. Taking pleasure with her, from her, but without joy.... Never with their endless voyeuristic stripping will they succeed in gnawing a thing to the point of its lack, stripping it bare, as a featherless man on the bank of a featherless river shrivels beyond even the shirt he doesn't have. For this, you need the desert: its naked, burning light. All at once. Without expecting it. To progress very slowly from it, not towards it. And only then: infinity, the cock crow...the joy of immensity released by the cockroach, by the outpouring of living matter from its body, as by the thick, devouring flow of water penetrating the bay seen from the maid's window in *The Passion According to G.H.* The greatest Spinosaurian book ever written, and necessarily written by a woman, since, as I told you, Spinoza is a woman. A woman who had Franny D's dream. 'One or several cockroaches?' asked Franny Lispector, furious. One cockroach and ten thousand lives. Immensity. From the window of the desert room, beyond the rocky gorges of Rio, favelas on a morro. Further on, the plateaus of Asia Minor, the Dardanelles Strait. Further still, the sands of the desert, the region of the great salt lakes, the Assyrian markets, the Egypt of the Pharaohs, ancient Athens, Constantinople.... For, while the Cartesian on rue Gay-Lussac, from the window seat of his bistro, can see no further than an ancestral arche-fossil deposit, the eye of the carioca cockroach sees through the very ancestral eye of the last troglodyte, and the oldest animal. And with this eye, it sees into the most distant future.

Like Cartesio, you expected explanations and, like him, you placed all your faith in this Polish vice-governor of the Dutch Tropics, Kristof Articzewski, who welcomed you there...since you have to rely on someone in the face of such a disaster, look for a helping hand. But this Christopher, this reprobate, will never help you out of the muddy waters of the river. This Articzweski or Arstixoff, as you like, will abuse you just like he abuses Cartesio. Because his own need is far greater than your need for an explanation. There's no need to swear that, as 'a man, a very manly man who loves women, of whom I have had many, I have never, ever, had such unnatural impulses!' Here you are, quite in love with this Artizewsque polak. But he is also the subversive agent who mixes everything up. It is he, to whom you open your heart, who is in truth the cause of all your misfortunes. He, the anti-Jesuit, the enemy of the reducers of the natives, the evil principle: the East India Company versus the Company of Jesus. He has no interest in making savages literate or Latinising the poor! He's just there for the loss of your humanity and, with it, of your entire civilisation. It's him, that anthropophagous giant with the head of a dog, cloistered as a child with Leminski in the monastery of São Bento, learning to track your most tenuous hopes. He, your Nordeste future. He, the demon who makes you think in circles. Ah, the fools who pride themselves on not thinking in circles and who have never met him! Too late, dear Bento. 'SpinoZa...Do you really think you can get away with sticking a Z in your name? Removing the Spanish E from Espinosa? Smoothing out your spines? What? What are you hoping for? What do you expect to achieve? I'm sorry, but this lover of yours is polonising you; your polak Z is all him. The becoming-Yiddish of Descartes. He who will take you back to Chechelnyk, from your first vermin-filled quay. He is also the demon decayer of Nordeste writing, who disorthographises Glauber's sertanejo language on the Eztetyke of the Kynema.

It is said in Brazilian school classes that
DEZKARTES, called to PERNAMBOUK by NASKAU
Settled in REZIFE
Where, every morning when he wakes up, dressed as a mãe-de-santo
He writes a long letter to a certain Bento
In an unknown Afro-Asian language
A Jew from AMZTERDAM who translates it into Latin and inserts it
According to a very sophisticated filing system
Of axioms, propositions, and scholia
Into an 'ETYK'
Which he plans to publish under the name SPINOZA
With a Dutch publisher
That is the truth of the matter.

Chaya Ohloclitorispector

For, contrary to what children are told, it is not by carrying children on his shoulders that Saint Christopher saves. It is not by giving free rein to his phoric impulse, *durch Nacht und Wind*, that he protects himself from the Ogre, king of the riverine alder groves where there grows a red wood covered with white or grey bark—the *pau-brasil* of the temperate zones. Contrary to what Michel Tournier thinks, it is not the superphoria of an astrophore child perched on the shoulders of a Nazi Gilles de Rais that rescues him from the Holocaust. The real Christopher, Tarado da Sé, the perverse giant nigromancer from Olinda, practises a different kind of medicine which has nothing to do with this deception, the so-called migration of souls, the crossing of the river to the other bank. It is an exclusively corporeal medicine. He does not shed his blood for the evening meal so that Roman blancomancers dressed in a chasuble sewn with gold and silver, after having thoroughly fumigated the room where their public is dozing obediently, can pretend every Sunday, at the appointed hour, to convert the cash, to transubtantiate the wine. The true Christopher does not bear the Christ who sanctifies through blood. Like the Devil in the Temptation of Christ in the Desert in Glauber's *The Age of the Earth*, the God of the Waters emerges from the ocean whistling the Marseillaise, he subjects us to the most terrible temptation, far more terrible than the temptation to use miracles: the temptation to love, to respond to his immense need, to his imperious demand for indifferent, total love. The temptation to be neutral, to be grey. The Claricean temptation not to cross over to the other side. To stay inside, inside the thing, the impersonal life of vermin; to stay in the mud of the river, on its third bank, without crossing over it. Who could resist such a temptation, the temptation to be as mediocre, as ugly as a small Nordeste salamander nestling in the muddy waters of a toothless mouth? To this extraordinary demand for divine love? To this demand of an immense, Neptunian God, *natura naturans*, simply doing everything he does in an infinite number of ways, none any better than any other? Without good and without beauty. Christopher is not a God-bearer, he is God. The God of SpinoZa. Of SpinoZa overcome by the temptation of *amor intellectualis Dei*...of SpinoZa tempted by his God. And it is once again He that Bento hallucinates at the foot of his bed: a giant Scabby Black God. *Deus sive Pindorama*. He himself beloved of God and loving God with the same indifferent love, furiously, joyfully neutral and grey...mulatto. And who, having given in to it once like Clarice, would not return like her, every night, covered in an ointment of flesh, to ride in the idleness of the night, until dawn, the shamanic horse of the king of the Sabbath, a winged quadruped emerging from the bowels of the ocean, an anthropophagous aquatic strix? To commit the most joyous of murders under the influence of the amanita mushroom? And to wake up in the morning by the stream with a mouth covered in blood? The blood of the victim, child or king, and his own, the living matter of the Sabbath. Ah, the humanisation of the humanisers! Who set aside God and the Evil One, Saint Christopher and Krystof, the Christ-bearer and the Pernambucan, the father's mount, *den Knaben wohl in dem Arm*, and the King of the Alder, the Devil of the Borders—the beautiful promise he makes to you to wear his mother's golden robes and to dance, dressed as a woman, surrounded by his daughters. No. There is only one mount, the riparian horse-strix, and it is he who devours the child, and the child who greedily devours himself on the horse's back. It is he, this Devil of Krystof, and not Jesus Christ, who sheds his blood—who, like Clarice's cockroach, sacrifices himself so that the substance of his blood may be applied, as a compress, to your eye, wounded by the tortures you inflict upon yourself. And so that your eye, by the medicinal virtue of this bloody slurry, may turn into the eye of a cockroach, a lizard. Polacopelophthalmotherapeutic OFÒ: 'So that you grow out of the body a new visual organ exclusively affected by everything that disorganises you. Just as the eye of the schizophrenic dreamer grows on the edge of the desert, detached from her body, affected in an infinite number of ways by the permanent disorganisation of people in trance. A feminine eye, exclusively feminine: olhoclitoris, rosebud eye, your Nordeste penis.'

Now you are on the side of the living matter of pleasure, having tasted the temptation of the neutral, of the decomposing mangrove, garden-city of the Devil, hell of Thule, populated by hypnotic pythons—'que me hipnotiza', says Cartesio—and reptilian monsters wearing Sephardic masks. Mouth full of living animals, knowing the taste of leeches. To have drunk the water of the fruits of stagnant waters, which according to Lévi-Strauss smell like a cellar, a smell from which he flees as he flees the black mud of the Bay of Rio, teeming with crabs, and the mangroves (of whose expansion he says that he cannot tell whether it is growth or decay). For it was not in Santos that Claude experienced the shock of the tropics. That negotiable shock of the tourmaline forest: the *thaumazein* which just makes the white man think more. The shock that leaves him standing there stunned, rattling off peculiar ideas about fossil matter, the Great Outdoors, the accretion of the Earth...via the subtraction of a tropical big cat revelling in the blood of a Black man as a Guayakí Indian relishes the vinous juice of a palm tree.... It is in Rio that the shock takes place. The panic-stricken perplexity of the European that prompts him to get back on board ship as soon as possible. The shock of the vermin, of non-fossilised ancestral life, the bicharada, there, alive, slowly stirring on the icy banks of the bay, staring at the intruder with the real eyes of Clarice's cockroach, the black and radiant eyes of a mulatto in agony, as old as the salamanders, the chimeras, the griffins and the leviathans—older than anything that any excavation, any drilling, could ever extract from the earth. The shock of *Catatau*'s bestiary,

in the face of which Cartesian logic fails, and to which Cartesio succumbs as one succumbs to the demands of too great a love. Life
looking down on you from the damp, coarse, living mire where there
germinates with unbearable slowness your identity as a civilised person, as a wise palaeontologist ready to go up to the pulpit in front of a
few dozen learned idiots to teach them that it is salutary for them to
think in their turn, in the first person, from the banquette of the bistro
where they will meet later on, that the world and its subtle architec-
ture exists without them. Without them! As if it were enough to get
back on board ship to put between oneself and oneself the distance
of a world-without-us, to overcome the olfactory intoxication of the
New World, provoked long before arrival by the fruity aromas of the
fermenting forest that float across the ocean to meet sailors, and to
replace this putrescent, vinous world with the world of the science
of objects petrified for millennia in their original, mathematical form.
It was to get the better of this rottenness that Claude, far from the
toothless bay, in Santos, removed the anthropophagous murder perpetrated by the jaguar, and the Woman of the Fantastic Forest, from
Le Douanier's paintings. As soon as he arrived, before he had even
met a single Tupi, Claude instinctively understood that if he wanted
to carry out his Brazilian mission without risking being cannibalised
by Brazil—without finding himself, like Pierre Fatumbi Verger, dressed
as a woman in a Salvador terreiro—then he had to be wary of the
Fantastic Woman, of the Parrot she wears on her arm, and of Jo, the
decapitated woman in *The Origin of the World* who, just like Cartesio, speaks to him in Polish, mocks him by imitating Articzewski. Of
Dina Hiffernan Lizpektor, who carefully prepares the manioc cauim
on the Sabbath nights to intoxicate the warriors and whet their insatiable appetite for cannibal vengeance. As all the Jesuits, Monteiro,
Anchieta, Gra, Azpicuelta, will tell you: there is no better image of hell
than the binge drinking of the indigenous peoples, ingesting unbe-
lievable quantities of alcohol, a catatau of all sorts of root wines and
fermented fruits, chewed in advance by the mouths of young virgins.
Because the realm of mould, the fermenting world, the realm of wine,
is first and foremost that of women. As is, in the end, the cannibalistic

hatred and the ensuing indigenous war. It was the same necessity that led to the forced enlistment of warrior-drinkers in colonial armies and the bottling of wines by merchant-growers. A Jesuit necessity: to prevent the intoxication of the pack by the ethylic fermentation of native plants chewed by women. There is no greater obstacle to the conversion of the natives than this natural, baroque, inconstant woman's wine which, like pau mulatto, is never the same colour, and constantly changes from one bouquet to another...only to be drunk before it has released its last fragrance. In contrast to the orderly armies of the Whites, where each man, reduced to the common gruel, sleeps, eats, and shits, indistinct, nameless and womanless, with all these other men, there is the festive din of the Tupi witches, where, under the influence of drink, exalted by the incessant singing and dancing, running around the village, the men recount the long list of their wartime killings and recover their memory of their names, their hundred names, their criminal names, all taken from the enemy.

Chaya Pinkhasovna Lispector's ancestors—Abraham, Isaac, Jacob, Judah, Tamar, Phares, Zara, Esrôm, Aram, Aminadab, Naassôn, Salmon, Rahab, Booz, Ruth, Jobed, Jesse, David, Solomon, Rehoboam, Abia, Asa, Josaphat, Joram, Uzziah, Joatham, Ahaz, Hezekiah, Manasseh, Amon, Josiah, Jechonias, Salathiel, Zerubbabel, Abiud, Eliakim, Azor, Sadok, Akhim, Elioud, Eleazar, Mathan, Jacob, Joseph, and Jesus, Jesus baptised by a rival Nazir, Yo'hanan Kristof Articzewski, and after all this time Pedro and Mania—how could they have believed that the Earth was created by God six thousand years ago? Because, I'm sorry, but they did. Six thousand years, the epineolithic, the age of the first Caucasian wine at Areni, and of the first names, the names of species and people, since there are no names without ethyl fermentation. The epinethyllic age when the meeting of the waters gave rise to the first humid fog conducive to the formation of grey rot on overripe grapes. Six thousand years, the age of the Serpent of Dreams, who was in the beginning, who was God, and who, with God, names all things and through whom all things are. The age of the cochylispector, the bufonidae, Latin-American batrachians, and the buphagidae, a kind of Mediterranean pitangua tic-tiui bem-te-vi, which proliferate in the century-old vine pastures of the Languedoc schist of Lenthéric, sheltered by the foothills of the Palaeozoic Cévennes. The age of the ruminants of the vines, tropical giraffes with deer antlers at Gers. The age of the blood pool, of the opaque pupil, extraordinarily reactive, surrounded by a large pink iris, which forms in the centre of the wine-making vats. Six thousand years: the age of Pindorama and Bicho do Fundo—which come after and are at the beginning. Fascinated as they are by the four billion and fifty-six million years that separate the accretion of the Earth from its balloon of red branco, perfectly protected against the slightest attack of acidity, the speculative realist cannot reach back as far as these six thousand years. Like Cartesio, Leminski's baroque cyborg, my dear Bento, and like the reader of *Catatau*, who is also Cartesio, you are now acceding to a totally new redundancy, a redundancy that is totally new...to absolute indifference, strictly identical to the most absolute information...the enumeration of all names, their epiphytic proliferation...Yo'hanan Hiffernan, Gilles de Ray-Lussac...the shimmering of one and the same image, the vision of a scabby black Brazilian, via a profusion of images, perceptions, and affects, Luso-Dutch, Syrian, Amerindian, Yiddish, feminine, vegetal, sexual. Zapped across at high speed. *Quo imago aliqua pluribus aliis juncta est, eo saepius viget* (*Ethics* V, Prop. 13). From the *Fort* to the *Da* of the ritornello put on record by Freud, it is always the same that returns, and from the *Da* to the *Fort* always the death of the same that threatens, the logic of education by stone, entirely based on the belief in non-existence, faith in an acephalous vaginal God—as if the tamandua could be missing, the stone failing to bloody the mouth! Complexity, like the complexity of wine, is not achieved by purification, but is born of a plunge into those depths of chaos where existence abounds, swarms, and proliferates. And each immersion is at the same time a blossoming. This is the other logic prophesied by Oswald, the Tupi logic, the logic of *Catatau*: the mutual exacerbation of immersion and blossoming. Not to mention: extroverted introversion, introverted extraversion. The mutual exacerbation of epic, unprecedented extraversion, an endless panoply of historical, geographical, and human documentation, and verbal introversion through the subterranean, inhuman channels of language and thought. The cyber-netic, recursive, disordered writing of *Catatau*, the most info-dense and redundant text ever written. Maximally informative, excessively diastolic, to the point of the most unbearable cardiac systole, the most acute cordial contractions: Katamenokata no monomio gatari, de kono, mono no oko mo kodomo condomino. *De Re Niponica*. VII 33. Inj. Judus. And thus maximally redundant: 0 = 0. The new language of philosophy, its Portuguese, the Latin of Descartes in Brazil in a state of tropical shock, Greco-Nipponese—an apocryphal, Afro-Asiatic Coptic Gospel Latin. The language of the priests of African India, of the kings-peoples of the Ember Island. Unreadable! Or readable only by an illiterate. In Yoruba?—'Àjáso n't'aáyán': the precise formula of the new Claricean logic. Exactly, the three hundred and fifty-seven ofò taught to Fatumbi, the eye of Sango, by his Babalawo teachers. To be pronounced after having pounded a certain number of flowers (banana tree), herbs (elephant's foot), grains and plants, an earth-worm and a bird feather (from an owl) with a lightning stone, having spread the preparation on pieces of red cloth tied to the four corners of a shroud, and having sewn it all together. So that was our work? Yes, that's it. The epineolithic crusher, the vermin...the feathers of the dog, the ubiquitous passerine...sewn together...that's it. The ofò that would be ineffective if not pronounced—it must be spoken! Writing or reading doesn't work. Unless perhaps written out loud...—and which, in order to act, to be the acting Word, must contain at least one syl-lable of the ingredient and of its action. And hardly form a sentence. Àjáso n't'aáyán. In the relatively informative language (in the French translation): *Àjáso*: 'To bring together the severed parts of a body'; *Àjáso n't'aáyán*: 'to cut in order to bring together is the characteristic of the cockroach'. In our new language, in the absolutely informative, hyperinformative language: *Àjáso n't'Chaáyá*: separassemble n't' Cla-farice. Bring back to life. The formula of the resurrected Heliogabalus. That's it! Do you finally feel (since it can only be felt), under the effect of this magic (since only the magic ofò provides it), what it means to 'sense that we are eternal'? Since your brand new redundancy, by disturbing your maniacal contemplation of a single Great Outdoors, finally awakens your visionary power as a Clitofaricean lizard: release a myriad of visions of a myriad of things, all singular, born from each other, without male fertilisation, by pure parthenogenesis. All these births, this vivacity, which are Guaraci's, here is your new redundancy, your absolute indifference, your neutrality, your grey colour, your brand-new mediocrity, eminently affective, positively affective, in the highest degree and in an infinite number of ways. It frees you from your passions through a Passion that is greater than you...the joyful affectivity of living matter, of its button-eye of Love, photosensitive and ophthalmographic, which, with its eight thousand nerve endings, meticulously registers the slightest optical refraction and immediately translates it into spasmodic pleasure. Because *quicquid intelligimus tertio cognitionis genere, eo delecamur.*

BENTO CARTESIO: Ergo sum, alias, Ego Renatus Cartesius, ca perdido, aqui presente, neste labirinto de enganos deleitaveis, —vejo o mar, vejo a baia e vejo as naus...vejo mais...

ARSTIXOFF ARTYZEWSQUE: Delicious Bento d'Amour....

Galli Mathias

'I asked a man what the Law was. He answered that it was the guaran-
tee of the exercise of possibility. That man's name was Galli Mathias.
I ate him' (Oswald). Born in 1797 into a family of wine merchants and
producers in Burgundy, like his older sister, mother superior of an
Amazonian Jesuit mission, and like his brother, Louis the Sixth, an
industrial wine missionary in the New World, Galli Mathias, a professor of political science with the Elder Sons of the Church, was serving
a grand mission of love: to open up a major diplomatic negotiation
between the peoples of the Earth and the Moderns who, like him and
his young friends, were finally trying to give a good account of themselves. Repentant Westerners who would be quite willing to confess
that they have never been modern, that they had never stopped
practising the same religion as other peoples, from the China seas to
the Yucatan, from the Inuits to the Tasmanian aborigines, the same
tinkering with idols and sacred objects, even if they did it differently,
because the same thing can be done in different ways—and theirs, the
Catho-Burgundian way, is not uninteresting...come and see for yourself! The greatest political project inspired by Vatican II, for the creation, in the form of a worldwide social media network, of an immense
Jesuit reduction which would start the catechetical work again from
scratch, without constraint, without violence, using only the seduc-
tion that our religion, our science, our philosophy, our law, would exert

on the aboriginal peoples convinced by the new missionaries of the G.M. Society of the perfect adaptability of Western practices to their own practices—of their aboriginal character! Positively aboriginal! The new pedagogy: colonial education by stone. Not sure it works.

Simulation of a diplomatic negotiation with Moderns who would seek to present themselves properly to other collectivities:

GALLI MATHIAS: Nothing at all different from what is already being done...

CUNHAMBEBE (with mouth full): Jaudra ichê.

GALLI MATHIAS: Ichê?

CHACHUGI: Aché. Cho, Cho, Cho!

STADEN: Ich. Ich.

GALLI MATHIAS: ...from the China Seas to the Yucatan.... The same matrix...

CUNHAMBEBE (to Galli Mathias): —Jaudra ichê!... Barkibia! Clear off! ARTYCZEWSKI (raising the stakes): —Idz! Idz!... Get lost, you spineless coward! Chicken! Shoo! Shoo! tè, tè, tè, tè, tè!...

LAMPIAO (playing the accordion): Oia eu aqui de novo...xa-xa.

CUNHAMBEBE, ARTYCZEWSKI, CHACHUGI, STADEN (in chorus, dancing around Galli Mathias): Xa-xa...xa-xa...

GALLI MATHIAS (in a woman's voice): Xa-xa...oia eu aqui de novo...cho- cho...oia eu aqui de novo...xa-xa...oia eu aqui de novo...chê-chê....

The proof? Poor Chachugi, up to his neck in bayja, busy since daybreak bending his bow, sharpening the hardwood points of his long arrows, with his back to the village, forbidden to see the woman, his wife and his child born in the night, excluded from the living matter, from the pink, vinous puddle, from the placenta...from the irritating blandness of the maternal womb he enjoyed...and all those jaguars that run up to him and summon him to enter the Fantastic Forest to compete with them for game, all those jaguars that invite him to return to the pack, to shed blood with them, to kill animals in order to recover his power to see the Woman, the marvellous apparition of the Fantastic

Forest, the only way for a man to be man, man-jaguar, vir-jaguar, to be man as the jaguar is man: spikes planted in the pulp of the living. Just as the woman in labour is man: a feline biting directly into the placenta—and to no longer run the worst risk of all: the humanisation of man, his masculinisation, the mortal risk of no longer being a jaguar, of being forever blind to Woman, of turning into a pane-papa, a jiji-cricri-fucking God the Father, the child born of a perpetual aplasmatic Virgin raped by her Son. For what the Tropics did differently was to have invented the Christian before the Christian was annihilated by the absurdity of the Tropics. To have already identified, long before Nicea, the Trinitarian madness, and long before Sophocles, the poison of the father-mother and the child. The divinity of the Father, the insurrection of the Son, the charity, the long-suffering, the helpfulness, the goodness, the self-control, the faithfulness, the projecting LOVE of the Holy Spirit. To have feared above all becoming a Christian—the greatest threat to the hunters' virility, their tropical virility, their jaguar virility, their crimson virility, bloody and vegetal, eminently feminine—their ability to turn jaguar, to turn woman, directly nourished by the plasma of living matter. But that morning, Pierre, the French chronicler of the Guayakí Indians, was really worried by Chachugi's silence. It was difficult to get a word of explanation out of his informant. And difficult not to sympathise, not to feel, right to the heart of his own existence—his Western, Oediplo-Christian existence, of course—the disarray of the masculine bending under the symbolic weight of Woman, forced to face the dangerously alive world of the Forest alone. All of this because of the child. So much unhappiness, so much silence, so much anxiety, it can only come from the child! The Son, the Separator, ready to rise up against the Father, to kill him at the first crossroads, to eat him up along with his brothers. The extraordinary coincidence of savage thought and the most powerfully self-controlled logos of Western thought. The unbearable silence of Chachugi as he prepares for the hunt, walled in by his unspeakable indigenous knowledge, firmly focused on succeeding in his conjuratory undertaking, bending the bow, entering the forest, killing game, can only be his way of speaking, his way of expressing the unconscious

savage thought that only gestures can express: the parricidal vocation of the newborn child. 'Savage thought, unconscious of itself in
so far as only gestures can speak it...'! Bullshit like this has to be read
to be believed! And written! When you read writers, all you'll ever read
is bullshit, and any writer, any man who, in the tropics or returning
from the tropics, knows nothing but how to write, as soon as he writes,
he'll inevitably write—the idiot—some bullshit. Unless you don't write:
unless you just try to fix what is most immediate in writing, try, like
Clarice, to fix, word by word, in writing, the very movement of this
frighteningly blissful saudade that merges against a woman's breast
'para sempre' and 'para nunca', for ever and ever, the instante-já, the
déjà of this, the d'jà of isto. To attempt a photographic, ocular, instantaneous writing of the already isto, ancestral and fugitive, briefer than
any word and longer lasting than any book. Unless, in the act of writing, one no longer has any other purpose or existence than the instant
of this. No other power than its power of metamorphosis. To make of
this 'ex-isto', this mode of being of the this, of being made up of it, of
being through it and in it, me, directly nourished by its substance, the
most appropriate or the least inept formula of my ego sum. To write
ex-isto. D'jáx-isto. Unless, like Clarice, but also Céline the lacemaker
of Asnières, you only write writing—just as, in order to really paint,
you must only paint painting. And to write it to you, my dear Bento.
To write writing to you, and to write it illegibly, writing Spinoza's Z to
you as one traces the outlines of a Yoruba odu in the powder of a
sacred preparation made of leaves gathered in the forest in the early
morning and solemnly crushed by bare-chested women. Writing to
you as the living Word writes, illegible only at the feet of scribes. By
writing, to take writing by the hand, for you, to write each word by
taking it by the hand. Feeling it vibrate. And placing it in your hand.
To make writing nothing more than a vibration of words without meaning, or with only auditory, bodily meaning. To write 'dinosaurs', 'ich-
thyosaurs' and 'plesiosaurs', and even 'spinosaurs', less to suggest
unconscious correspondences, secret exchanges, than to increase,
now, on the spot, our own oculo-clitoridian quivering, and since the
clitoris is an eye, a hearing-eye, to reach out as close as possible to

the point at which writing will turn into seeing, this very seeing of the eye through which life sees itself—the point at which meaning will be exclusively corporeal. Unless we use writing to sustain the shock of the now, against the grain of that German melancholy which, through writing, entirely subtracts itself from that shock. Or better still: to provoke it, to go to the Tropics, to multiply moments, aromas, to free up their sequence—even to the point of risking losing the reader, even to the point of risking information in the most absolute sense. Even to the point of risking no longer being read at all. At last! Heard only by an eye. Galli Mathias will never succeed in symmetrising us. Because Pierre doesn't want to hear Chachugi's silence; he can't hear it. Because his silence, his early morning concentration, truly free of all moods, he cannot endure it, any more than he can endure the ordeal of isto, wanting instead the mortal flow of moments. Its incessant silent flickering, its lethal-vital appearance-disappearance. Like Staden, and all the unpalatable philosophers of cold countries, he is afraid of death. So he writes. And, of course, he writes a load of rubbish. Nonsense about masculinity and femininity, about the Guayakí twofold equation: man = hunting = bow, woman = gathering = basket. About how it is impossible for a man to lose his right to the bow without his having to carry the basket. About the sad condition of the man forced to perform various feats with the bow or else he will fall from grace and be forced to join the women's group, to really become a gatherer-housewife and therefore to 'metaphorically' become a woman, like Krembegi, the Guayakí homo, the *kyrypy-meno*, the anus-lovemaker, who no longer cuts his hair, never catches another animal, but makes the most beautiful necklaces from teeth that women wear when they are happy. If Krembegi is pleased by this happiness of the women, it is of course because he has in a sense accepted his forfeiture. With a wise stoic resignation. At least one must assume so: for Krembegi, like Chachugi, is not very talkative, and, being a very manly man, the Frenchman certainly does not envy him his homosexuality. That is why he will never write his writing to you, my dear Bento. And, not writing it to you, he will not see what writing cannot hope to comprehend: that Krembegi is not a metaphorical woman, but a real woman. That her homosexuality really fulfils, in the feminine, the feminine and the masculine. That only a homo, like Heliogabalus, or Spinoza resurrected as a woman, can be a priest of the masculine, of REAL masculinity. Krembegi may have swapped the bow for the basket, but he has not lost the sharp point: the jaguar's claws, the shape of which his hands, with fingers spread and folded, will take to the grave, the paca tooth with which he pierces monkey canines one by one to make the beautiful necklaces that women occasionally wear around their necks and always at the bottom of their basket, and his tiny coati penis, coaticloris, which the Aché hunters compare to the barbs on the tips of their arrows. Points upon points, points par excellence. These do not point to any meaning, but to life alone, to the naked, ex-isto life of the living. By piercing it. In order, through this piercing, to gather the juice and marrow, the nourishing matter of the living. In order, through this piercing, to truly feed on this matter, exclusively so—just as Clarice pierces through the cockroach's shell to the white matter in order to eat it, and just as the Aristotelian-Cartesian carapace of the *Ethics* can be pierced to get to the pau mulatto of Bento's hallucination in order to feed the eye. For although the women do not kill animals, the substance they collect in their baskets, gathering the larvae of the forest and the soft brains of the pindo palm to grind them together into a thick soup, is nevertheless the same substance that the jaguar hunters pierce with their bows. The same organic, viscous vibratile gum, guar gel, in which she who writes writing for you manages to fix the instante-já, the instant-ichê/ cho, déjà-l. The material in which she makes the print of her native panther paw, the signs of the já-guar odu. Krembegi is a priest of the masculine because he has understood: that in order to be a man, it makes no difference whether you are a hunter or a gatherer; that by abandoning the masculine for the basket, he was instead fulfilling the masculine through femininity. How different from Chachubuta-wachugi! The Indian who is strong enough to hunt, but who, having lost his bow, unable to fire arrows into an animal, catches coatis by hand, chases armadillos into their burrows, wants to go with women, *heim gehen*, but not to be a woman, not to pierce holes in monkeys' teeth, not to harvest vegetable matter—but whom no woman wants. No, Galli Mathias will never succeed in symmetrising us. Because Krembegi and Chachubutawachi are absolutely different. Because the Guayakí Indians have already understood the difference between themselves—hunter-gatherers of living matter dedicated to piercing the hard matter of the species of the forest-world, indifferent to the social, phallic difference between the masculine and the feminine— and all those, over here as well as over there, who, like Chachubuta-wachi, are incapable of sharpening a point and going into the forest alone to track down a howler monkey. For lack of courage, of course, but also and above all out of idiocy, out of being unaware of it, and who still hold on to their masculinity to the exclusion of the feminine, have their photograph taken as hunters with a dead animal in the basket, and who, like Chachubutawachi, wear as ornaments on their manly chests, tied onto a string, the untranspierceable objects pro-duced by the white man's industry—a bullet casing, a dozen bottles of penicillin, a few keys from sardine tins...objects donated or left behind by the missionaries for the amusement of women and chil-dren. This idiot Chachubutawachi, this 'Great-pig-savage-with-a-long-beard', this marrano-savage, this clownish guayakí, this hybrid which is ridiculous in that it distorts the masculine from its meaning of being a woman, that's what they want to make you into, my dear Bento. You, who know nothing but how to write and yet, all the same, strive through writing, from the very heart of your idiocy, in Latin and *more geometrico*, to resemble Krembegi—to resurrect Heliogabalus! You, who strive for a homo form of writing—as homoZexual as pos-sible. Galli Mathias will never succeed in symmetrising us. Because the Indians had already invented Galli Mathias, Gallinaburgutawachi, the Modern who wanders among his people, his feet in the anthro-pological matrix, proudly wearing around his neck the Industrial Object, the finest achievement of the Whites, the totally manufactured Sacred Object with its Made in Paris chic, infinitely indebted to the most Catholic Portuguese slavers for having rightly described it as a feitiço, the facts/fae-tishes of the Negroes of the Guinea Coast, and the Orishas of Candomblé too, if the ethnographers are to be believed, if they are to be read that is, since Galli Mathias only knows how to read, not like Bastide, still reeling from the shock from the tropics, and certainly not like Fatumbi Verger, who cannot be read but can be seen, and seen with his own eyes, which are the very eyes of Sango—the one who sees and knows everything. Pierre Fatumbi, the bem-te-vi ethnologist. The exceedingly Catholic Chachubutawachi of Sciences-Po is even capable of making Whites believe that by allowing their fabrications to proliferate, to the point of confusing the natural with the human, they are doing neither more nor less than the Negroes of Africa or Bahia—that by fighting their own industry through philosophy, by using thought to widen as far as possible the gulf between nature and culture, the animal and the social, mektoub, they are still working toward their hybridisation, toward the same industry, themselves ending up by producing sobjective, humanotural monsters—Kant, Hegel, Husserl, Heidegger, Lacan, Derrida, etc., all African sorcerers, adorned with junk necklaces, penicillin teeth, tin teeth, shell-casing teeth, but, of course, without power, without Aṣẹ, *kraftlos*. Beautiful symmetry! The most daring form of White diplomacy of all time: presenting yourself to others as being just as harmless as you imagine them to be! An original invitation from the Quai d'Orsay, addressed to all the Ixés, cho-chos, and xa-xas, to do the Chachu, to celebrate the feast of the New Paraclete, of the Symmetrising Spirit of the West and East India Network, an English-speaking Pentecost, necessarily, since Chachubutawachi the Basket-Hunter cannot take part in the nocturnal songs of the Bow-Hunters who, in the heart of the forest, invent languages that no one speaks. However, Mae Senhora had warned Gallichachu: 'Beware of Verger, he is a sorcerer, he has powers!' Galli Mathias will never succeed in symmetrising himself with Chachubutawachi. If he had seen, had just seen, Pierre Fatumbi's snapshots, he would have seen that the magical work of Candomblé does not seek to transform the raw material to make Objects as beautiful as a shell casing; it prepares the material but without ever transforming it. He would have seen that the African Negroes of the old Slave Coast, like the Brazilian Negroes of the Bay of All Saints, are indeed black and scabby, and do not make or sell anything, but involute into this primitive matter without regressing into it, this grey powder, Iyerosoun, of medicinal and liturgical leaves gathered in a wild place, bush or forest, known only to hunters familiar with Ossanyin, the god of leaves, primordial, untransformable mud, a mixture of vegetable substances kneaded in the blood of sacrificed animals. Without this vital matter, nothing would be done...that isn't done. Even Patricia de Aquino says so. An initiate is not asked 'What divinity are you making?', but 'você é feito de que santo?' He would have met Aroni, the little man missing a leg, perhaps Clarice's third leg, smoking petun from a snail shell stuffed with his favourite leaves through a hollow stem, and Nana, the goddess of swamp mud. Both of them would have taught him to do nothing, to stop feeding his Object factories with exotic material torn from his peoples, and to simply let himself be made of it.

Jean-Baptiste-Théodore-Marie-Rosalie Botrel

Do we even know what Antonin Artaud is suffering from? Even his acupuncturist, Soulié de Morant, has no idea. From the electrodes shoved up his ass, into his mouth, and into every other fucking hole they could find? From pissing out all his blood, being liquidated, like diarrhoea? The white shits? White and ugly? Is he suffering from the asymmetric warfare of the Whites? Who kill without joy, purely for the sake of it, without first plucking and painting their victims, without first getting drunk with them on the women's drink, but just with a bullet in the head, quickly, by the side of the road, or more slowly, with repeated blows, right in the flesh. Without expecting the enemy to demand to be stunned by a sharp blow on the head, having himself already stunned so many of our relatives and friends, certain that vengeance will be visited upon all of us by all of his relatives and friends, who are equally doomed to death by his confession, so that only a healthy and solid enmity remains between them and us. Does he suffer from the asymmetric warfare of the Whites, who leave the bodies there, piled up in the middle of streets or at the bottom of pits, or burn them, in short, who do not know what to do with them, and who above all demand that we reconcile, that we become good friends again? Who, for fear of death, at the slightest trifle, kill their best friends, make them their worst enemies, so that only friendship remains and nobody comes back to kill them. Which, you must understand, my dear Bento, requires real carnage, gigantic massacres...unimaginable piles of inedible red meat. Does Artaud suffer from friendship? Could be. And do we even know what it is that the Indians care about, what they hold to? Because that's what it's all about: what costs him the friendship of the Whites. Compressed, crushed into the ground by an extreme heaviness, senseless and as empty and free-flowing as a witch's womb. As mineral and volatile as the New World according to Claude. In short, stricken with shellshock, experiencing astasia-abasia, unable to walk, to stand upright, to cross the great water that separates him from the Land without Evil. The colonial disease par excellence. The shock of barbed wire. This is exactly what the war did to Nijinsky when it robbed him of dance. The white trauma which, on 19 January 1919, made him dance terrible things, floating above a pile of corpses. The dance of Saint Vitus, choreography of the Cold Lands. The collapse of style, the loss of what keeps the skeleton and the spine upright, of what keeps the flow of words going, of the e-ry mo'ä a of the Mbya singers of Hélène, Pierre's wife. Look what they did to me, my dear Bento: they carried me to the baptismal font before I could even stand upright and gave me a name that did not stand me up straight on the floor of their church. They carefully wrote it down in all their records to remind themselves of that which cannot be remembered orally: my restless name, my bipolar name, the one that you just have to shout to throw me shaking to the ground. But you, you gave me a scabby black Z. A cunning, sonorous, Polish letter. You invented me a tropical, Tupi, oriental God, Karai Ru Etê / Karai Chy Etê, to receive my name and my voice, as well as my origin. And all languages were mingled in it. Amomoût latu as tatkwe terik'ejá aáyáns minajáso, tamo daleko tamo anusun usunu sina minajá, waiwi lapa-yawii ãwe ayiajá nd'ndá-wasu àjìyè nd'ná-ti dìde n'lè. If Galli Mathias had taken the time to listen to Jeanne Flora-Bocaine-Saada, the anti-witch from Mayenne, perhaps he would have known, like Eduardo, how to answer the Myrtle's question about what the Indians hold to, and which is not made of stone—since nothing is held together by stone. But Galli Mathias is in a hurry to get back from the tropics. To get back to work. To forget all that and to take up his post at the

Factory of Objects, of Ideas, of everything that can be hung around the neck to make the Chachubutawachi—the Universal God Fazer, the Godfather of all peoples from the China Seas to the Yucatan, from the Inuits to the aborigines of Tasmania. Surely we're not going to symmetrise natives with peasants from Mayenne—Minor with minor!—when we have far more modern, far more presentable Moderns in reserve? Kant, Hegel, Lacan...If only. The Babins, Jeanne's peasants, are obviously far less attractive...they even have a certain way of acting the native that risks blowing the whole thing wide open. A slightly awkward, handicapped way, as a Modern might, but terribly accurate: asking Jeanne to invent mortal enemies for them from scratch, only to regain their vitality and secure the rest of the world for them. It's easy to see why the Indians are so keen on their drinking and their wars! Just imagine having so many enemies, so much hatred, so many murders and murderers' names without even having to consult Madame Flora. How different from the Babins, who immediately confuse their ethnographer with a psychotherapist and talk to her for hours about all their misfortunes in great detail. Whereas Chachugi and Krembegi are silent. They have nothing to say to Pierre. That's what Whites are like. They build dams and then they build salmon ladders along the rivers. They even put the fish in vats to transport them by truck to the spawning grounds. A whole system of reparation, costly and terribly effective, to do what isn't done—doesn't need to be done. For sure, it will make them flee the other collectives, from the China Seas etc., peoples without enemies obliged to seek counsel in order to hate, to cure themselves of friendship. Because there is no other way to be yourself than to get out of yourself, no other way to stand up than to walk, to go and meet your enemy to kill or capture him and take his name. No other interiority than a permanent movement toward the outside. No other identity than the continuous migration toward the coast, the march toward the edge of the Ocean, on its edge, under the guidance of the song, the voice, ñe'e, which keeps it upright. The Land without Evil toward which the Guaraní walk is not a goal or even a horizon—it is the very Land of the walk, the terrestrial Land upon which the song keeps a people upright. If you walk, you're walking into it. Even Hélène, Peter's wife, finds it hard to understand this, finds it hard to see that nomadic disorganisation, the deadly march, is the only thing that holds, the only thing that is held to by those who hold out. It is true that White people always migrate sedentarily, crossing from one shore to the other, sitting, looking for new friends, eager to erect their stone temples on the new land. And then what? Is there a more suicidal migration than that of a person who, in order to travel, takes a plane that he might as well not take, because he has nothing really essential to do where he is going, but he takes it anyway, knowing full well that he is going to die in the air, just because there is nothing really essential stopping him from packing his bags, going to the bank, taking a taxi to the airport and getting on the plane? If the Indians of Brazil migrate across the Earth by walking—so long as they are not forced to get up to go to work or to go to the bank to withdraw their meagre wages—and if the Europeans migrate in caravels, both nautical and aerial, invariably following the same route which, starting from Lisbon, takes them along the African coast before heading for Recife, it is not, to put it in the language of the philosophers, because of a difference in 'transcendental categories'? For, if we are to be precise, there is no other 'transcendental' condition than the walk that keeps one upright. The German masters of the 'transcendental' will tell you: their business is to find out under what conditions a man can be *Selbstständig* and *Unabhängig*—free-standing and not suspended in mid-air. Walking, singing, and killing are all part of the same movement. An exclusively anthropophagous movement. One and the same murderous and prophetic march toward the nourishing enemy, which insurgent peoples sometimes miraculously accomplish, and of which certain European national anthems still bear, albeit shamefully, the trace: 'Qu'un sang impur abreuve nos sillons', may an impure blood water our furrows! May Rosalie, the bayonet that is 'so pretty', that 'pricks, and pierces and cuts', that 'pierces at the head and drives all the way through', may the 'polka dancer', 'so ruddy and dewy', 'pour us the impure blood of the Boche to drink', the infantrymen of the Great War still sing, so as to put their hearts back into their chests while the

German shells fall. But Jean-Baptiste-Théodore-Marie Botrel, the lyricist of 'Rosalie', the Karai of the trenches, can't do anything about it. The piercing has been lost once and for all. The shells rain down, and generations of survivors suffering with abasia will parade at regular intervals to the shrink, who will dewitch them by discovering symbolic enemies and give them back something like a walk—although leaving them with a slight but incessant tremor in their hands that will render them forever *pané*, preventing them from piercing the eye of a bird in flight with a single stroke. Unless they escape Oedipus, like Anani, Jean Camp's Languedoc Empedocles, by throwing themselves head first into the warm, purple must of the wine vat, into the moist, sticky flesh of the shifting pool where the grapes dance their infernal round, swarming with millions of worms. But they rarely go that far. In the absence of Karai, of real singers capable of leading them by the force of ñe'ë porä, the beautiful indigenous words, on long, murderous migrations, they rely at best on smooth talkers, teacher-therapists, *Wissenschaftslehrer*, professors of knowing-how-to-know-how who teach them the practical rudiments of the *Bestimmung des Menschen*, the vocalisation of man, and use pretty words to get them in the mood to set out on the road. Some of these fine speakers, like the Saxon J.-G. Fichte, even reach a certain degree of perfection. Not in the sense in which Hélène understands the Guaraní aguyje—'the perfection which, by means of asceticism (*sic*), makes man exist as *logos* (*sic*) by giving him access to a knowledge (*sic*) whose power (*sic*) alone is henceforth sufficient to animate him (*sic*)'. Not in the Greco-Latin sense, then. But in the Indian sense. By uttering, for the sole benefit of his apprentices, in the intimacy of the seminar, an unwritten and illegible word of initiation, exclusively oral and almost unintelligible, by giving rise to fantastic and sonorous visions made up of preposition-words and verb-actions that improvise out of the bloodless, debilitated elements of White philosophical understanding a violent drama that leaves nothing to the *Begriff*, to the clawless hand of Chachubutawachi who claims to be able to kill without piercing but knows nothing except how to pick up a dead animal from the ground—*Sein*, *Träger aller Realität*, *Grund*, and so on.

Because the Whites know the formula. Once they've made sure that someone is willing to close the door, and also the windows, their therapists in knowing-how-to-know-how, once they are well and truly shut in, deliver the formula with the utmost precision. The formula of IMPOSSIBILITY. Get in and get out, at the same time. Get as far away as you can, and come back as close as you can—very, very close indeed. Separate yourself from everything, isolated in the centre, and disappear everywhere, disappear, evaporate into the cosmos. Fleeing in a straight, endless line, and concentrating on a finite point. But do both AT THE SAME TIME. One through the other. The formula of the anthropophagous, entropiphagous march, of nourishing disorganisation. The formula for the production of time, of the impossible-já, dead and resurrected, of the instantaneous separassembler where the past and the future originate. In short: the formula for the continuation of the world. Who gives a fuck about the socius...whether it's organised or disorganised...the formula for the CONTINUATION OF THE WORLD, for the CONTINUATION OF PINDORAMA, for the whole world that they are, the world that is. No matter how well they know the formula, they don't know what to do with it. They may lock themselves away to talk about it, merely to talk about it. Sometimes they may even do so in the largest of conference rooms, shouting about it to a big audience, but they can't stop writing it, and reading it, and writing what they've read about it. And what they write and read is a crock of shit. Utter bullshit. I even knew one of their students, a crazy girl who wanted to call me mummy and who understood the Mata Atlantica as a vast expression of love! My friends from Nantes and Bordeaux, probably due to some kind of Batavism, were infatuated with this chronic lover of mine, who was always keen to adopt the smallest piece of rubbish, collecting and cherishing hundreds of empty bottles, abandoned toys, bits of scrap metal and lost objects on the shelves of her orphanage in Montmartre, a stone's throw from the Place des Abbesses. No doubt they recognised in her the Chachubutawachi they had met in the heart of the rainforest and who had reassured them so much about themselves...and loved them so much, so pas...pas...papa...passionately....

Davi Kopenawa

Davi Kopenawa once saw the God of the Whites. Teosi. The one whose twisted words know only threat and fear, and nothing of the Forest. Well, maybe he saw him. We don't actually know. Because in reality, even with the yãkoana powder, no one has yet managed to bring down his image, to see him dance. All the same, what Davi saw that day, the day he died because of the White man's epidemics, the white shit, that white shit dog that devours your belly and crushes your bones, is something like what the spirits call Wãiwãiri, a being with flabby, luminous skin that dances on the spot, agitated with soft, frightening shivers. Powder never makes you see that! Even the old powder, the soft powder! To see it, you don't have to die of gunpowder, but of xawara, the White man's disease. If it weren't for measles, influenza, malaria, tuberculosis, and worst of all the xawara plague fumes hungry for human flesh that the Whites spread over the Forest, the fumes from the ores they extract from the Earth, no one would ever have seen anything as terrifying as this type of *Verklärung*...and Sesusi trying to reassure you, the deceiver, after having scared you to death. Look how it pisses him off, Momo, the soft powder, the dead cumrag. And how it strikes a white man, even from North Africa, the hot cum, the live powder. It's so unstable that he doses it out carefully so that it doesn't blow up in his face, jà, but always afterwards, so that it only explodes very locally, on little paper sheets, hung on the walls of a

Museum of Modern Art in a Dutch colony in the New World—or better still, on the pages of the exhibition catalogue to be read at home, in a limited edition, surrounded by Objects, all cherishable and subtractable at will, all made of matter torn from the Earth and the Forest. Great Art. The problem with the Whites is that they hold to their debilitating abasia, their visual asthenia, as tightly as the Indian holds to his walk, but in a different way: without holding. Always suspended in mid-air. This is why they systematically translate the formula of impossibility into floating, and the world, their world, they imagine and create through floating, through the suspension of a continuous hesitation between form and formlessness, contour and infinite line— they also say: '*de.tɛʁ.mi.ne*' and '*libʁ*'—and for all vision see only transfigured beings, soft-skinned Wãiwãiri, *schwebende Erscheinungen*, faces of luminous cloth, like Giotto: an airplane-kite-Christ, but never a scabby black Brazilian. Out of their own feebleness, because they see nothing but themselves floating, and nothing but floating, they are constantly migrating, over the sea and through the air. That's why Peter, James and John, the terrified disciples of the Mount Tabor religion, risk their lives boarding the transatlantic caravels. And fall vertically. Pulverised. Turned into news items. They sew or glue together loose skins, covered with drawings of beautiful words, to make Books in which they hold them captive and torture them. When, like Clarice, they can't or don't want to improvise them directly in their writing—which is very difficult, and which the philosophers, who are usually smoky, are usually pleased to find smoky. I read one of these books so much that the knots that held the skins together wore out and broke, so that its leaves flew again. It was written by a white Russian, a graphomaniacal former swimming champion who was having a friendly argument with a fine, clear-eyed Jesuit about what to make of the beautiful words of a certain Jean-Amédée Sapinette—a famous German-speaking French philosopher who, at the time, was the talk of the town in every talking shop in the Latin Quarter. Because one feels stupid not to do so, I myself had slavishly covered page 100 of my Russian book, roughly translated from German into French, with drawings of words. This Articzewsko Parisite explained—in an almost unintelligible language, peppered with incoherent German words, difficult to interpret, because ethnography is a really difficult science, especially the ethnography of Whites—how, therefore, for a European White, to meet-together (*tsu'zamen'trefen*) and to take-by-hand (*auf'fasen*), is the same thing. That all their strength (*kraft*) lies in this handshake, and that, by the magic of this handshake, this strength is infinite, that it is their infinite acculturation-force (*''ain'bilduns'kraft*), of themselves and of other peoples. And above all that the product (*pro'dukt*) of this force consists precisely in this famous *'sve:ben*, between swimming (*'svimen*) and weaving (*'ve:ben*): progressing in a fluid element, never on Earth, passing a weft through the crowd without having first stretched the warp between two wooden sticks stuck in the ground; in general: without ever stretching, spiralling or weaving anything—neither bow nor basket, as foreign to both as Chachubutawachugi. Difficult stuff! My Philonenczewsko explained how, for them, thanks to this *Schwab-utaschweben*, this migratory smoke that the Whites produce by means of their force of acculturation, there is a time, a time that they are also able to suspend for a while, by suspending the use of their force, but not for too long, a suspension of their suspension in the air, what they call *er'ha:benen*, their way of remaining upright, lifted in suspension above the Earth, in a kind of sublime, celestial, and solemn erection which astonishes them greatly and gives them the most delightful shivers. But most of the time, unfortunately, between these moments of suspension, they cross the Oceans. And their migrating, epidemic fumes cover the Forest. The underneath of the first Sky, which once upon a time fell, they pierce and rattle it with explosives to extract mineral oil. And in turn, they also shake the new Sky, the one that thunders above our heads, hastening its fall, since in the end they know nothing other than how to fall and how to make everything fall vertically, all over the place, and their only legacy to the world is a series of miscellaneous facts. Everything that spreads through epidemic fumes is acculturation: footballs, flu, cans and bottles, measles, credit cards, shoes and trousers, malaria, philosophy books and prayer books, everything that spreads through ideas, realism, idealism, materialism, gallimatism. Objects, diseases, and ideas: the same lethal fumes. And then also all that passes through, sneakily, on the side, in the salmon passes they build after having smoked out the country: forbearance, helpfulness, solicitude, kindness, fidelity, the AIME project. Because they don't love themselves. They don't love their own kind. They only want what's best for others, and only on condition that they have first annihilated them, by the hundreds of millions—two hundred and fifteen million, to be exact, as of 11 October 1492. For lack of enemies. And how many scabby black Africans? They don't like their friends. They run away from them. They leave them there like Mrs. Berenge, the caretaker in *Death on the Installment Plan*, the old fool. Like the silly, ugly girl in Rue de l'Acre. And Louis-Ferdinand's grandmother, full of hatred. They all go far, far away into oblivion, changing their souls, the better to betray. But what do I care if they listen to me or not? So long as you're there, my dear Bento. And who else would I write to? And how can I write down everything that comes to mind in such a mess? How would I capture what comes from behind the thought without thinking about it? How, old woman, would I be full of milhares de passarinhos barulhando? If I didn't write my instantaneous notes to you? See how the estranger, the Horpays, the epidemic gold digger, here as everywhere else, walks all over the paths made sacred by the footsteps of the ancients, mows down the mature tree, tears out its roots and, finally, cuts the forest edge to edge as if it were a single tree! Hear him cry out his glory in the combes in palauras that nobody knows! And so many want to become White, to lick lo cuòu of the estranger! To be his valet, to be his bitch! Even Gilles-Plateaux, my dear Bento, the French philosopher of Millevaches, no longer speaks the language of Marcela Delpastre, confuses a tree with a book, doesn't like the Tree and the Root, prefers invasive rhizomes. When Marcela's toothy mouth of granite, a thousand veins open, bleeds onto the land and into the sea. Bleeds and sows in lands that are far beyond the sea. Plants its seeds and roots from its heart, across the ocean, a tree of words, aubras palavras, which blooms as a Yanomami song tree blooms in the New World: in a thousand mouths, singing tirelessly, without ever repeating themselves, in all the languages that can be invented, magnificent melodies as innumerable as the stars in the bosom of heaven. And a thousand trees of beautiful words, covered with a thousand singing lips. The thousand song trees from which all music is drawn. Without which the world would have no music. On both sides of the ocean. For, having copulated too much, they have come in great numbers from abroad to kill the country. But no matter what they do, the country never dies! For ever, the living sap rises from one side to the other. Never before have so many leaves and so many fragrant flowers been produced. Having copulated too much, having eaten too many women's vulvas, the poor people, here and over there, have had to wall themselves and their children up, feeding them the cooked flesh of our own children, our women and our elders, encased in iron or plastic tins, which they prepare in huge numbers and keep to eat later. And that's so that later they can crate up their own dead, whose meat, fed on stainless matter like this, no longer decomposes—but which nobody eats. Strange kind of cannibals. They also put their feet in boxes made of skins and fabrics. Some kind of mania. The women's breasts, too, they put them in two more or less opaque boxes tied together, pressed against the chest, and tightened at the back with a small lock. The skin, their skin, they refrain from covering with drawings and, once the soft parts have been held in place, curiously, they cover themselves entirely with sheets of flabby skin, woven from transformed materials, vegetable, animal, or mineral. In fact, the manufacture of these soft sheets is a major business, mobilising armies of slaves in their colonies. Except for their faces, exposed to the poison of their industrial fumes, which naturally sag and droop beneath their eyes, darkened by constant activity: prospecting, extraction, transport by air and sea, processing, transport by air and sea, storage, transport by air and sea, trade— which is exhausting. Because they don't stop until they have exhausted the world. When they are tired of hunting us down to eat our hearts out, they build houses of stone paste in the middle of nowhere on the land of the dead country, which they offer to us with great ceremony. But they don't have it easy. Sometimes Indians who have come from Egypt with Sara the Black tear up the floor of their houses, rip out the cement, expose the living earth, scare the vermin, open a field right in the middle of the dining room, dig a hole where they can light a fire, and pull the string of a violin between two fingers to teach the children how to sing the beautiful words and make the girls dance. If you don't want to lose your bearings, the best thing is to stay on the path, to stay on the right path, to thank the gadje without accepting anything from them. No houses, no tin cans, no balloons, no books, no ideas, no realism, no idealism, no empiricism, no materialism, whether speculative or historical, whether transcendental or not...who gives a fuck?

Glauber Das Mortes

I am afraid. Gadjos normally know nothing of fear. They are only afraid of death. Otherwise, they are fearless. Each one stronger than the next. In the buildings where they store their most precious Objects-and-Ideas, they organise jousts between themselves and themselves, inventing singular battles between enemies who have never met, never touched each other, battles in which no blood is shed, but which attract a crowd of strangely animated young men and women—not driven by a thirst for revenge, though. All around them, in the streets and down to the quays...even further away, Negro people, grassboys, hygienboys, bottelboys, gutterboys from Abidjan, dockers, porters, labourers, smugglers from Accra on the borders of the Slave Coast, are busy before their blind eyes. When they finally see what these people are doing, only then do they become afraid. As I am now afraid. Like a child prostrate over having killed another child...out of stupidity. Sad gadjos. Jean Rouch, the Quai d'Orsay's documentarian-emissary in the dark continent, puts the camera down as soon as the glossolalic pantomime turns sour, and goes into hiding as soon as the Blacks in a trance attack the dog, rushing with drooling lips to slaughter the poor beast and drink its raw blood. The Whites talk a lot about the Blacks. But few care about what they do on Sunday evenings in the suburbs of the colonial city, what Mountyeba and Moukayala do when work has stopped. They spare themselves from knowing exactly what they do to the Blacks. The Haouka sect! Can you imagine, my dear Bento? That's like saying: 'the Xawarari sect'! The Mad Masters of Epidemic Fumes and Objects! Mountyeba High Priest of the Order of Chachubutawachi...that's the way to look at it. A mixed-up mess, a real *galimatias*. Instead of bringing down the images of the xapiri or the orishas, they call upon the deities of the Whites, the gods of the City and of Technology, the spirit of the loco-motive driver, the spirit of the governor, the spirit of the captain's wife...the spirit of the Coloniser. No, but can you believe it? They find me amphigoric! Unclear! Not well-knitted enough. And look at this mess: a Black religion of the gods of colonisation! No wonder Moun-tyeba and Moukayala meekly return to work on Monday morning. Jean even sees it as a model of mental prophylaxis for White proletarians. Are you kidding me? After deliberating, since the gods of Civilisation deliberate all the time, arguing endlessly about what we're going to do and what we're not going to do, they decide to cook the dog to eat it later with the friends back in town. Gilles listens to Fanny. But not only that. He listens to everyone and anyone. Without thinking too much about it. He doesn't know that Glauber, in *Wind from the East*, does a bit of whoring in passing, though he's not enough of a clown to let himself get caught up in the folklore of the gigolos in the unforgettable Mai français...just out of affection for a skinny, bald and sad forty-something filmmaker, tired of poetry, totally inoffensive. Ah, Glauber's friendship, my dear Bento! The bourgeois, moralistic and serious anarchism of Jean-Luc and Dany, Gilles takes it at face value, and when Glauber makes the signpost of political cinema for a pre-tentious white Russian chick—'this way to unknown cinema, aesthetic adventure and philosophical speculation! This way to Third World cinema, a dangerous, divine, marvellous cinema!'—Gilles takes it seri-ously and Third World cinema, that of Glauber and also of Rouch and Perrault, becomes the modern political cinema. A real can of worms! And all this because of the dog, the moose and the porpoise, the anomalous animal, the luminous beast, the 'marvellous' animal, as Stéphane-Albert says. But what's so marvellous about preparing canned dog meat, trapping a white whale and trucking it to an aquarium in New York? Does Gilles know what Glauber saw when he watches *Wind from the East*, the Good News he spread back in Brazil? He saw the corpse of the suicidal Godard up close: the dead image of colonisation! THE DEATH OF COLONISATION. And you, my dear Bento, did you see the death of colonisation? A aristocrato-anarchist French philosopher, cloistered in his apartment, taking at his word what a depressive Swiss anarcho-right-wing filmmaker has to say about Third World cinema to a toothless Brazilian pole who has no interest in the destruction of the West, its religion, its morals, its philosophy and its cinema, but only wants to BUILD, to continue to make cinema in order to build his Land of Embers in sound and images. Like Céline, Glauber does not like destroyers. He is a builder. Seriously? Yes! That is also the death of colonisation. This way that Michelangelo has of writing and reading everything and anything about the Accretion of the Earth, the Metaphysical Other, the Inexistence of the World, the Foreclosure of the Name-of-the-Father, Class Warfare, the Constitution of the Moderns, the Lack of a People, from one end of the planet to the other, on TV, on the net, in the press, in San Francisco on a skateboard, on the Great Wall of China wearing a chapka, in a shopping mall in Rio—Gavea?—rather than going to paint the Sistine Chapel. Or inventing the infernal bazaar of tropicalism. Neither Godard, nor Rouch, nor Perrault film blood, or provoke the viewer. They are without violence. There is barely a trickle of blood on the white back of the porpoise trapped by the Whites of L'Îsle-aux-Coudres at ebb tide. A trickle of blood you could easily miss. When Glauber Das Mortes REALLY wounds a Carnival cangaceiro to death, when he REALLY revives the hungry violence of St. George in the desert, of Oxosse-Museau-Sale, that old negro from Lampiao, the Scabby-Black-Saint-Guerrier, on a Parade day, and exhibits the images and sounds of this REAL violence in the dark rooms of the temperate environments where Gilles locks himself up for days on end with his hat screwed on his head, Grand-Louis and Stéphane-Albert, the fictioning actors of Pierre, great-grandson of Breton pig stickers, are still waiting for the Achab, the Genie, the Achabutawachi who will be able, to capture a porpoise without hurting it too much, to bring the back of the Moon down to earth, to bring down the image of the Absolute, to make Teosi tremble above their heads, his luminous shadow floating on the surface of the waters—slightly streaked with blood...on the right side...far from the heart. Gilles marvels at the porpoise fishing done by the Tremblay family, the followers of the Grand-Malouin, the illustrious Inventor of Terres Neuffves, the Precursor of the French Antarctic. He marvels at this, Gilles, in his darkened room at the Champo cinema, his hat screwed on his head, while Franny stays at home to watch her documentary on wolves...a wolf, wolves... you really must see it! Boneless meat. Smooth and white. Luminous. Totally decerebrated. Not a brain in sight. And it still stands up! All by itself. Magic, magic! That's what Gilles likes about Cézanne: the erection of the flesh, the vertical positioning of the soft parts, the stance of the fluid, the turgidity of the uterus. While Frannytoris dreams at the edge of the pack. That's Gilles's style, his own brand of columnialism. He gets it from Charcot's priapic girls. All it takes is for a very-manly-man doctor to set them up, with astasia-abasia, right in front of a camera, so that every time they do a contortionist's act, contractures and oscillations, a beautiful bow-without-organs, a bow-body, a rod-body that doesn't shoot, full and smooth as an egg, a body-egg...a harmless, intensive, inoffensive bow, no longer anything to do with piercing-killing...a bow for Chachubutawachis...made to measure. Perhaps that, my dear Bento, is what white people call *fal.lys*: this penile uterus, this hysterical position of the penis, which they contrast with the all-too-organic penitoris of women, the eye at the bottom of their belly which they dread so much out of fear of losing the only thing they care about: this worshipful wavering between turgidity and flaccidity.

Saint Bento

When the girls of the waters, the Iara, seek to attract young boys using amorous magic so as to lead them into the forest and under the surface of a dark lake to their father, Tëpërësiki, so that he can teach them the songs which, by naming them, enable them to cough up the evil beings, the Whites powerfully clasp the child in their arms and accelerate the fatal course of their steed through the night and wind. When a young boy is visited in his sleep by the xapiri, his arms adorned with scarlet macaw tails and a profusion of brightly coloured feather bouquets, coated with vermilion annatto dye, and he awakes screaming, terrified by the beauty of this invitation to share the secret of the spirits, they stuff him full of Chamonix Orange and, so that he doesn't go mad, any more than he already has, they take him once or twice a week to Meudon, to Colette, a good friend of Philonenc-zewsko's, a philosopher who makes it her business to desensitise male children by teaching them to be more interested in the vulva than in what they see at night. This is why the Whites never know the saving words. They are defenceless in the face of their own epidemic fumes, mortally wounding themselves with every move they make to free themselves from the miasma. They are unable to bring down the spirits that know how to repair the sky, and are heading for disaster. Help me, Saint Bento, help me, Old Negro, to cough up my fumes! It takes courage and experience to stand upright, even when twisted. There's no point graduating from the School of Dead Languages, being fattened up with mandarinades and examinines, wearing the infantile feathered bicorn of the quays of the Seine. You don't have to be so cosy. I know this well, I who was born by accident in someone else's cradle—in a basket woven to hold someone completely different from me. I, who was so nervous, REALLY nervous, with such a serene, painless and happy nervousness, that they had to give me a nervous disease to keep me asthenic in the cradle. Symmetrising and standing are now one and the same thing. Galli Mathias has no idea. I say 'now' because it can only be done now, if we hold the present moment firmly—religiously—in our hands, the very moment when we die together, now, you and I, my dear Bento. I will only be able to stand, now, if I join together our two asymmetries, my absolute difference from you and your absolute difference from me, and hold them together, faithfully painted, as only Clarice can, on the two doors of one and the same gate, but (listen to me carefully now) strictly identical to each other—to hold and see together, painted identically on each of the gate's wings, our two absolute differences, differently different, since you are as different from me as I could ever be from you. For the sole purpose that our asymmetries should meet at last. May your image appear to me and, since we are both painted identically on the two doors, may my image appear to you as the image of a scabby black Brazilian dancing at dawn by the bedside of a Luso-Polish philosopher, as the image of a bem-te-vi bird singing in the bloody dawn on the quays of a toothless bay, of a Fantastic Woman charming snakes in the depths of a World-Forest, of a Nordestine Witch riding at night, covered with a flesh ointment, of the horse of the king of the Sabbath, of Fatumbi-Descartes dressed as a woman in a Salvador terreiro...of everything that is denied by those who have the audacity to claim they can reach reality without magic...just by racking their brains. This, my dear Bento, is the morning prayer that I write (precisely!) to you.

Fifteen
Concluding Points

1. *A Scabby Black Brazilian* is the story of a flight, of the invisible *becoming* of an academic French ego, devoured by Brazil under the influence of two eminently equivocal encounters: that of a Carioca anthropologist, Eduardo Viveiros de Castro...and a spirit of the Amazon rainforest that appeared at the involuntary instigation of the former in the guise of a Japanese-Guaraní translator-devourer, Takashi Wakamatsu.

2. The author of the *Brazilian* is João Pyaguachu, a man with a good heart...João, the subject of a joyfully and lovingly consensual anthropophagic murder.

3. The *Brazilian* is an account of the kidnapping of a fac-zenda professor from the sertão-rainforest to a semiotic Quilombo, undertaken by a heterogeneous, shifting, and aberrant collective, a world of characters and writers, friends, and enemies, assassins and poets, who are more or less recognisable, or in fact rather unrecognisable. Here the totality of the French academic episteme, the colonial hegemonic model of the French University, (finally) manages to completely collapse in a roaring burst of laughter.

4. The *Brazilian* is an unreadable book.

5. The *Brazilian* sits on a bookseller's rack, on the edge of a shelf, among all the other books, just to serve as objective proof that it is still possible to free oneself from being attached to the disastrous epistemic regime of the printed book, which, by force of arms and colonialism, has secured its ignorant grip over almost the entire surface of the Earth....

6. The *Brazilian* is a disaster. A cargo plane crash. Catatau. In the sense that the Melanesian 'Kago' is a parodic metaphor for Culture. The crash of a French plane that Melody Nelson never got on.

7. The *Brazilian* is a tale of rotting in the forest: of becoming-earth, becoming-humus—the decomposition of meaning, writing, and reading.

8. The *Brazilian* practices a literature of the rainforest, tropical and dense, a literature of the mudflats.... That tropicality which in Latin America, Africa, or Oceania means, primarily, the anthropophagic consumption of the White Man and his Reality within multiple realities, the metamorphic Natures of the rainforest where everything gets mixed together.

9. Beneath each word, beneath every damned arrangement of statements, swarms a whole horde of vermin that digs in deeper, decomposing, swallowing, and shitting out all the lexical and grammatical material of language, making the liquid and gaseous substances of thought communicate...prompting Lévi-Strauss, the academic of the quays of the Seine, to get back on board his boat, disgusted, poor fellow, at the disgusting sight of fertile decomposition in the mangrove.

10. It is said on the banks of the Congo that the members of a tribe crushed by a ruthless government were transformed into monkeys by their ancestors to preserve them from evil. The *Brazilian* is a monkey-book: written in an almost private, unseemly, exceptional language, it definitively frees João from the tax of written meaning, of the signed concept, of the conventionalisable exception that the urban, Western,

and modern culture in which he was educated/destroyed demands of him in order to constantly reinvent himself.

11. The *Brazilian* is a book registered under the code 978-1-915103-08-6, filed under 'Political science', 'Philosophy', 'Anthropology', 'Fiction'.

12. But the *Brazilian* firmly keeps its international publishing and commercial barcode in check, generated as it was with a certain amount (a catatau) of silica, gold, palladium, iron, aluminium, lead, zinc, nickel, tin, silver, platinum, mercury, cobalt, antimony, arsenic, barium, beryllium, cadmium, indium, petroleum, copper, selenium, sand and Teflon—all of which materials are accumulated by exploitative extraction. Since it cannot be exported as transatlantic cargo, it sends Pindorama's gold back to the belly of the earth.

13. The *Brazilian* is a merrily wicked and wickedly merry book that has won the contempt of the imbeciles of its author's homeland, true patri(di)ots, on all sides of the Atlantic.

14. The *Brazilian* is a realist book that tells the true story of Bento de Espinosa, Franny Deleuze, Dina Lévi-Strauss, Chaya Ohloclitorispector, Galli Mathias, and all the other conceptual personae across history about whom the Academy has ceaselessly spread utterly false information.

15. The *Brazilian* tells the true story of Descartes, who was ordered over to Pernambuco by Nassau and who settled in Recife where, every morning when he woke up, dressed as a Mãe-de-santo, he would write a long letter in an unknown Afro-Asian language to a certain Bento, a Jew from Amsterdam, who translated it into Latin and inserted it, in accordance with a very sophisticated system of classification, using axioms, propositions and scholias, into an *Ethics*, which he planned to publish under the name of Spinoza, with a Dutch publisher.

And that is the truth of the matter.